TEARS OF THE INNOCENT

PALESTINE: BEAUTIFUL EVEN IN SORROW

RAMSHA RAIS

This book is dedicated to all my brothers and sisters in Palestine, Sudan, Syria, Somalia, Afghanistan, Lebanon, Xinjiang, Rakhine and Kashmir, who have been alienated by the rest of the world.

Contents

Contents

Preface

The Prophet (p.b.u.h) said that if the whole world gathered to help you, they could not help you, except when Allah decided.

And if the whole world gathered together to hurt you, they could not hurt you, except when Allah decided. So am I afraid? No. Should you be afraid? No.

And The Prophet (p.b.u.h) said if you see evil, then change it with your hand. If you can't, then change it with your speech, if you can't then hate it in your heart.

So here I am, trying to change it.

Acknowledgements

The more books I write, the more grateful I become to the people who encourage me to write everyday. My friends and family and mentors, who taught me a great deal of things. Their actions, their love and their words encourage me to metamorphose my feelings into words so that it can be read and more than that, felt.

A quote from Little Women, that makes me want to test new limits everyday.

> *"I am not afraid of storms, for I am learning how to sail my ships"*

CHAPTER ONE

THE ICE-CREAM TRUCK

Ahmed Qaradawi came running out of his school and his eyes lit up as soon as they landed on his father, who was patiently waiting to be recognised by his adorable 8 year-old son.

"Baba", shouted Ahmed, running towards him and the first question that rolled out of his tongue was,"How is Halima?"

Mahmoud laughed and picked up his son,"She's exactly how you left her in the morning. Infact, she's been crying for her brother, all day".

Ahmed chuckled at his father's response.

Halima was Ahmed's 7 months old sister. She was the cutest little thing he had ever seen. After the vacation, he didn't even want to go to school because that would mean having to leave her side. That would mean, taking a break from seeing Halima sleep, smile and play. And he couldn't afford to do that.

He was in a hurry to get to home but it all dissipated into thin air when he heard the bell. A familiar sound. A bell that rejuvenated his senses and lit a tiny spark in his eyes and ecstasy tugged at the corner of his lips as if invisible fairies playing tug of war. He turned his head towards his father and looked at him with longing eyes.

It was the bell of the ice-cream truck.

Mahmoud immediately passed a hand over his pocket to check if he'd have the money to pay for the ice-cream, before giving Ahmed any further hope and then nodded at him.

"Okay go on, choose one", said Mahmoud, putting Ahmed down on the ground and seeing him run off towards the ice-cream truck with jubilation.

Mahmoud Qaradawi had been married to Maryam Abdullah Ubaid for 17 years and had 4 children- Ahmed, Saleem, Fatima and Halima.

Ahmed was 8 years old and his sister Halima was 7 months old and their older siblings Saleem and Fatima were 14 and 16. They didn't live extravagant lives but they weren't destitute either. They were satisfied with everything that they had been blessed with. And never for a moment did they stop thanking God Almighty for all that they had.....even when they didn't have a lot.

CHAPTER TWO

GOING AWAY

Another booming sound and Ahmed flinched.

"Baba",he cried, looking towards his father who himself was sweating profusely and held his tiny daughter in his arms. "Why hasn't Fatima come back yet?"

His mother, Maryam stood in the corner with Saleem and said in a calm voice,"Don't worry Ahmed, she's safe somewhere"

The family was at home when the bombings started, again. Unfortunately, Fatima was out, at her friend's and she hadn't come back yet. She had talked to her parents and was advised to stay there until it was safe to come out. It wasn't safe out on the streets. But it wasn't safe in the homes either. Buildings kept falling. People kept dying and Ahmed couldn't make sense of any of it. What was happening? Why were people being murdered? But all he got as an answer was another missile.

He had heard that his friend Omar had died with his entire family. Just a week ago, they were playing with marbles and laughing. Ahmed hadn't known what death truly meant. Even when his grandfather passed away, he was 3 and it gave him an idea that death is bad. People cry when someone dies. No wonder so many people were crying now, Ahmed thought.

"Will I not see Omar ever again?",asked Ahmed, looking up at his mother. For some reason, she started crying and nodded her head.

"You will meet him *In sha Allah*",said his mother. "You will"

Mahmood checked to see if Halima was comfortable in his arms. He then got a phone call and he immediately picked up. He looked stressed while he listened to what was being said and he responded with,"We will meet you in 10 minutes".

"Where are we going?",asked Maryam, looking at her husband.

"We have to evacuate. It's not safe here. Abdul and his family will pick us up and we will get Fatima and get out of here",said Mahmood.

"And go where?",asked Maryam.

"Out of here. Just.....out of here"

His eyes reflected hopelessness but he still pulled on a brave face for his family.

"Pack whatever is important. Keep the bags as light as possible",he announced and went into the other room to pack all the important documents after handing Halima to Saleem.

"Mama",whispered Ahmed, barely audible.

"What is it Ahmed?",she asked, not looking directly at her son because she was so busy collecting the essential things in a bag that had flower prints.

Ahmed smiled because it used to be his favourite bag. Not anymore. Not after this bag would remain imprinted in his memory as the bag which they took before their house was blown apart.

"I am hungry Mama",said Ahmed.

Maryam looked guilty but they didn't have any food. Atleast not right now.

"Just hold on for a few more hours Ahmed. I promise we will get you something to eat",said his mother and found a container in which she kept dates. "Have this for the time being. It should keep you full for now".

Ahmed and Saleem gratefully ate the dates, thanking Allah for that particular blessing. Thanking *Allah* even after there were missiles being dropped all around them. Because indeed, he tests his strongest soldiers.

CHAPTER THREE

FOUND

Fatima was nowhere to be found. They rode their van to the place where Fatima was supposed to be at. The building had been demolished.

Ahmed could see people carrying off some people in their arms. He could hear their screams and their shouts which only made his little heart beat faster. He looked at his mother for support but she kept shouting his sister's name and grabbing strangers and asking if they had seen her. Even his father was panicking. He was shouting Fatima's name and helping a group of people move some rubble where there were supposed to be people under that.

Mahmoud could only hope that his daughter was safe under that rubble. How ever much safe a person stuck under rubble can be.

It took them ten minutes to move over the bricks and the rubble and rescue a woman who was frantically searching for something to cover up her head.

"My hijab",she screamed as Maryam rushed to her aid with something to cover up her hair while the men respectfully lowered their gaze.

The woman got out and so did two other boys who were related to the woman but Fatima could still not be found.

"Mama do you think...do you think she-",Saleem began but Maryam cut him off.

"By *Allah*, Saleem don't say another word. Allah will have protected our Fatima. She is safe somewhere. We are not going anywhere until we find her",said Maryam and as if in answer to her words, they heard a frail "help me" from underneath the rubble of the middle portion.

The men immediately heard it and ran to her aid. They were successful in rescuing Fatima from under the rubble but her condition was worse than other people who they had rescued from under the rubble. A piece of rebar had found its way into her abdomen and was embedded there. She was losing blood, fast.

Ahmed was terrified at the sight of that.

"Mama what is that thing on Fatima?", screamed Ahmed, pointing at the rebar sticking out of her abdomen, and crying.

"We will get it fixed. We just need to get her to the hospital. They will fix it",said Mahmoud, putting on a brave face.

He carried Fatima in his arms, careful not to touch the piece of rebar or move it, to prevent any further blood loss.

He carefully placed her in the van and they drove to the hospital. Her breathing had slowed down but she kept reciting an ayah of the Holy Qur'an, over and over again. Her mother kept on reciting another verse from the Qur'an and wiping tears escaping her eyes. As Ahmed was trying to take it all in, they reached the hospital. They got her a bed and waited for some time before a doctor was available. He examined the wound and looked stressed out.

"We will try our best", he consoled the crying parents. Saleem was holding Halima who had woken up and was crying in her brother's arms. Ahmed was quiet but his heart beat was fast. He just wanted Fatima to get well. If she didn't heal, then who would help him with his homework when his school reopened? Who would tease him and make him giggle and laugh? All these thoughts crossed Ahmed's mind as he watched his sister, lying on that bed, in pain. They were escorted outside and were told to wait while the doctors did their job.

CHAPTER FOUR

A NIGHTMARE

All around them, bodies were coming in and blood was everywhere. The smell of blood was very strong and made Ahmed quite uncomfortable and dizzy.

"Mama what is that?", asked Ahmed, looking extremely scared and holding his mother's leg and trying to hide behind her.

A man walked in, holding two small decapitated arms in his hands and cried as he handed those arms to a woman who was already wailing. Those arms must have belonged to some child who was Ahmed's age. The child must have used those arms to write, to ride a bicycle, to play, to eat. But now, they were just decapitated bloody arms, separated from the body of its owner.

Ahmed's mother immediately tried to cover her son's eyes with her hand but Mahmoud held her back.

"Let him see",he said, with a trembling voice. "Let him see what they are doing to us."

"Who is doing this Baba?",asked Ahmed, now crying."Who is so cruel?"

"Israel",said his father as if that one word was supposed to explain everything. As if that one word was supposed to be a reasonable explanation for all this chaos and destruction.

"Why are they doing this? Did we do something to them? ",he asked, fearfully

"No....we didn't do anything",said his father, with pain in his voice.

The doctors came out of the room, but Fatima was still in pain, with the piece of rebar sticking out of her abdomen.

"We will have to operate and try to remove the piece of metal, before it damages her internals any further. But we do not have any anaesthesia. She will have to be awake throughout the process. She will feel everything, all the pain.",the doctor informed the father who looked agitated. He kept looking around, as if trying to find someone to cling on to, for comfort or trying to find a door, which once he walks out of, will prove that it was all just a terrible nightmare. But it was all real. As real as Ahmed looking at his father and for the first time seeing tears in his eyes.

"Do it, do the surgery",said Mahmoud, finally, after a lot of consideration.

CHAPTER FIVE

THE O.R

After a while, Maryam agreed with Mahmoud and they both told Fatima about this who was expected to be reluctant but she was infact, quite willing and eager to have that rebar out of her abdomen as soon as possible.

"It will be fine, *In shaa Allah*",said Fatima, who looked like she was barely holding it together. "Just get it out please"

Her face was pale due to all the blood she had lost and she kept staring upwards, reciting a certain ayah of the Holy Qur'an while the doctors did their jobs, the place was as sterile as it could be. Everything was cramped up and even Fatima's parents were allowed in the operating room because she was holding on to her mother's hand during the procedure. Ahmed had somehow snuck inside the room too, even when he was advised to be with Saleem, who was taking care of Halima outside.

The doctors were doing something that looked extremely painful, to Fatima. They were trying to get that piece of metal out of Fatima's stomach. Ahmed wanted to scream at them to get away from her but he knew they were only trying to help her. He could see Fatima, shutting her eyes as tears welled up from deep inside and flowed outside her eyes and clenching her teeth at times, when the pain got worse, she just recited the shahada in a louder voice, instead of screaming.

"Why is Fatima reciting the shahada? Is she going to die?",wondered Ahmed, as a solemn tear fell down his cheek.

All of a sudden, there was a lot of movement around Fatima, and they started shouting things in technical terms that Ahmed just couldn't make sense of. A lot of blood was coming out of the hole where the rebar was stuck. The doctors were trying to get the bleeding to stop while Maryam, whose face was shining with tears held Fatima's hand harder and rubbed it and said to her daughter,"Come on, don't give up yet. Dont lose consciousness Fatima. By Allah, stay with me".

While Mahmoud stood by helplessly, the doctors tried to do everything they possibly could, to help the young girl who was bleeding to death on the operating table. Ahmed couldn't take it any longer, he ran towards his sister and cried,"Don't leave me Fatima, please don't leave me"
The doctors didn't care if a young boy had just entered into the O.R. They were trying to stop the bleeding, which seemed impossible.

Fatima turned her face towards Ahmed. Ahmed flinched. His sister's face was ghastly pale. She opened her eyes one last time, looked at Ahmed and smiled, she then looked above him. Although there was no one standing behind Ahmed, Fatima stared and she opened her mouth to speak. Ahmed leaned in closer to hear what she was about to

say. And her lips parted as her final words escaped her tongue,"*Ash Hadu anla Ilāha Illallāh Wa Ash Hadu anna Muhammadan 'abduhu wa Rasuluh*"
Fatima's father understood and he put a hand on Fatima's head and said,"Give my Salam to Prophet Muhammad."
Fatima managed a smile at her Baba one last time and her eyelids dropped.

CHAPTER SIX

A MARTYR

Everything was quite a blur for Ahmed after Fatima died. He remembered leaving the hospital with his family, with Fatima in his father's hands. For some reason, his father wasn't crying as much as his mother. Saleem was crying silently while Halima was crying very loudly, although Ahmed doubted that Halima was crying because of the same reason as they were. The baby was probably very hungry.

Ahmed remembered burying Fatima and then looking at his sister's face one last time. Why did she look so beautiful? She looked so much at peace. And her body, it smelled so nice. Ahmed couldn't really describe it but it was unlike any *Attār* (perfume) he had ever smelled.

Ahmed remembered his father saying she died a martyr and Ahmed didn't know what it really meant but he guessed it was supposed to be a good thing because his father smiled after saying it and his mother nodded and smiled too.

"What is a martyr?",asked Ahmed before he could stop himself.

Ahmed's father put a hand on his tiny shoulder and said,"A *shahid* (martyr) in Islam is someone who dies in the way of Allah. A martyr will not be tested in the grave, nor will he be punished in the grave. The martyr will not feel fear on the Day of Judgment"

"And Fatima is a martyr?",asked Ahmed.

"Yes she is",said Mahmoud proudly and added,"*Walā taqūlū liman yuq'talu fī sabīli l-lahi amwātun bal aḥyāon walākin lā tash 'urūnn*"

(<u>Translation</u>: Never say that those martyred in the cause of *Allah* are dead—in fact, they are alive! But you do not perceive it.)

"Can I be a martyr, Baba?",asked Ahmed innocently.

"*In sha Allah*, Ahmed",said Mahmoud.

That's all Ahmed could remember and then he woke up inside the van, his head was on his mother's lap and his leg was on Saleem's lap who was holding Halima. She seemed calm now, staring out of the window.

"Where are we going?", asked Ahmed.

"We're going to someplace where bombs won't fall on us.",said Mahmoud in response to the question.

"I haven't prayed *Maghrib*, Mama", said Ahmed, looking up at his mother. His mother's face was swollen but atleast she wasn't crying as much now.

"I know, son. We'll pray as soon as we get there",replied Maryam and put a hand on her son's forehead, pressing her palm against it and moving her hand through his head which sure made him smile and forget his world crumbling around him, for a little while.

CHAPTER SEVEN

Unfriendly Nights

It was a cold night and Ahmed wasn't particularly joyful at the prospect of spending it without any blankets or pillows. It was just them in a tent, with a mattress.

"Mama can't we atleast get a couple of blankets? We can share",said Ahmed groaning.

"Ahmed, don't be ungrateful! You atleast have something over your head and a mattress to sleep on. Many people don't even have that",said Maryam snapping at Ahmed.

It was night time and they were currently staying in a tent which Mahmoud had set up with the help of a few friends who had set up their tents in the same row.

Ahmed noticed, under the light of the only lit candle in the room, that his mother's face was puffy and her eyes were swollen and red. She had been crying again. Probably while she was praying.

The five of them slept together and Ahmed refused to sleep anywhere other than beside his mother. He couldn't sleep without sensing her presence nearby.

Even when Mahmoud blew out the candle, Ahmed stayed up.

"Saleem, are you awake?",asked Ahmed in a low voice.

Saleem, who was sleeping next to him gave his monosyllabic response implying that he was indeed awake too. "Yes"

Saleem had always been the reserved kind of boy. He was a bit of a taciturn person, always keeping himself guarded and uncommunicative . He was reticent about his feelings too. He was, infact, too much of an introvert, in simple terms. Everyone assumed that Saleem was a cold, impertinent person but Ahmed always knew that his brother was just extremely shy. Infact, Saleem hated the cold. Ahmed was actually surprised as to how Saleem was quiet and not whining about how cold it was or how he had nothing to cover himself up with.

"Do you think our house is still there, Saleem?",asked Ahmed.

"Maybe"

"When all this is over, will we ever return back there?"

"I don't know",replied Saleem

"Are you scared, brother?"

"Are you?"

"A little",said Ahmed and then waited for a while. "Okay no, I lied. I am scared..... I'm very scared of the people bombing us...."

"Dont be",said Saleem. "We should only ever fear the creator. Not his creation."

"But we could die",said Ahmed

"So what?",said Saleem, wisely. "Every being has to return to Allah one day. If He decides it's sooner for us, it's probably better. Dont you know that death is not the end? It's merely an end to this life. But in the Hereafter, you'll enjoy"

"But we won't be able to talk to each other if one of us dies", replied Ahmed

"Who cares? We'll join each other soon enough",said Saleem smiling in the dark.

He then realised that Ahmed would probably get scared from that answer, so he added,"In heart, we'll always be together, brother"

"But Fatima isn't with us",said Ahmed mournfully.

"No, she's not",said Saleem. "She's in a better place"

"Does the place have ice-cream?",asked Ahmed.

The comment made Saleem snort and turn his head towards his brother and whispered,"Sleep now"

CHAPTER EIGHT

THE CAMP

When Ahmed woke up to the smell of bread being made, it truly made him realise how hungry he was. He had woken up for *Fajr* to pray with his family but he'd immediately gone back to sleep afterwards. His stomach grumbled in response to that smell. He turned to see that his mother and father were outside the tent. His father was fanning a fire, on which they had kept a big metal pan-resembling thing. And his mother had rolled up dough into thin pieces and was cooking them on it.

Saleem was nowhere to be found when Ahmed looked around inside the tent. He saw Halima fast asleep beside him, which made him happy. He forgot all about his problems and his hunger and edged closer towards his sister.

She was sucking on her thumb, even in her sleep, she smiled sometimes. Ahmed wondered if she was having a wonderful dream. Was Ahmed a part of her dream? He often wondered that. He kissed his sister's forehead and she smiled again.

"I love you so much", whispered Ahmed, smiling at her. He doubted she'd be able to hear him or even understand what the words "I" "love" and "you" meant, together. But he hoped that she understood how much her brother loved her.

Ahmed pondered how heartless a person would have to be in order to muster up the courage to be willing to hurt an innocent little soul like her. He was sure that if anyone saw her, they wouldn't be able to control themselves from kissing her soft chubby cheeks or from holding her in their arms.

"Ahmed are you awake?", came Maryam's voice from behind him interrupting his chain of thoughts.

Ahmed turned around in answer to that.

"Dont wake up Halima",warned his mother.

Ahmed nodded, got up and went outside the tent. He noted it was sunny and he also noted that he kept getting hungrier by the second. He looked longingly at the bread his mother was making.

"Go look for Saleem",instructed his mother. "Then we will sit together and eat"

The mere usage of the word "eat" excited Ahmed. He'd get to have food. Oh what a delight.

"Where did he go?",asked Ahmed, immediately wanting to summon Saleem so they could skip right to the good part. The part where they would eat.

"He went over there, to help others distribute the flour",said his father, pointing at the other end of the camp.

Ahmed nodded and ran off.

CHAPTER NINE

HOMEBOYS?

Ahmed expected Saleem to be found easily but it proved to be an impossible task. He went around asking strangers if they had seen a 14 year old boy, wearing a light blue t-shirt, around here.

None of them could identify him. But finally he stumbled upon a young boy who looked like he was the same age as Ahmed, holding a football.

"Have you seen my brother? He is around 14 years old and he was wearing a t-shirt.....a sky blue one",asked Ahmed, looking at the boy.

The boy looked like he was processing his question.

"Night sky or day sky?",asked the boy

"What?",asked Ahmed, bewildered.

"The colour of the t-shirt,you said sky blue...so what sky",replied the boy

"Day sky, light blue",said Ahmed, in a matter-of-factly voice.

"Yes, I did see him. He was the one who delivered the flour in our house today",said the boy.

"Oh, where did he go after that?",asked Ahmed.

"Why do you think I would see where he was going?",asked the boy

"I mean...I was just asking you if you did see where he went",asked Ahmed

"Oh yeah, well, he went that way",said the boy pointing towards the other side of the camp.

"Thanks....you could have just told me.", said Ahmed and then smiled at the boy."You're weird"

Ahmed meant it as a compliment and the boy took it as one.

"I know",he said. "My parents are dead"

That was totally uncalled for and Ahmed was shook. Such a young boy, without his parents. How was he surviving? Why was he not crying? So many questions popped up inside his tiny little head. Ahmed couldn't imagine living without his parents. He just knew it was impossible to live without them.

"How did they die?",asked Ahmed

"Snipers shot them",replied the boy, then he smiled and said,"Atleast they aren't hungry now"

"They were hungry before they died?",asked Ahmed, starting to feel bad.

"We hadn't gotten food for more than 2 days almost and whatever they were finding, they kept feeding me and my sister with it. So they didn't have anything for themselves", explained the boy. "And then they died as martyrs"

"My father told me that martyrs are very lucky people", said Ahmed, proud that he knew that.

"I know",said the boy.

"Are you living with your sister now?",asked Ahmed

"Yes. She's the only person I have....and my football",said the boy

Ahmed laughed,"A football is not a person"

"Not to you",replied the boy.

Ahmed now confirmed, that the boy was a weirdo, said,"What's your name?"

"Ali",smiled the boy.

"I am Ahmed",he said. "And I should go now, I was supposed to be looking for my brother"

"Okay",said Ali. "Will you come around? We can play football together"

"I don't know how to play football",Ahmed confessed.

"I can teach you",smiled Ali, hoping with all his heart that Ahmed would agree. "We can be homeboys"

"What's that",asked Ahmed

"Its another name for....friends"

"Okay, I live in that tent",agreed Ahmed, pointing at his tent.

Ali nodded and Ahmed turned away to go.

Ali just couldn't contain his excitement. Afterall, he'd just been successful at making a friend here.

CHAPTER TEN

SEARCHES AND GAMES

When Ahmed went back to his tent after a solid 15 minutes, he found Saleem there.

"I was searching for you!",complained Ahmed as soon as he looked at him.

"And we were searching for you!",said Saleem.

And then after a while, it was made clear that Saleem had returned to the tent 5 minutes after Ahmed had left, which rendered all the efforts that Ahmed put into finding his brother, useless.

All of them sat down to eat the only thing his mother had prepared. Thin pieces of bread.

"I made a friend today", declared Ahmed happily.

"Really? What's his name?",asked Maryam looking kindly at Ahmed.

"Ali",said Ahmed. "And he plays football. He said he could teach me. Can I go after I finish eating?"

Maryam looked reluctant. She didn't want to let Ahmed out of her sight. She knew it was a safe zone, here. No possible threat could harm them here but after losing her oldest child, Fatima, she was extremely scared of losing another one. She couldn't afford to lose another child to this genocide.

"I don't know Ahmed....maybe you should stay near here, okay? Not go too far",said Maryam with uncertainty.

"It will be fine Maryam",said Mahmoud, interrupting. "We are safe here, don't worry. Let the kid have some fun."

"Okay",said Maryam, looking back at Ahmed. "But not too far"

"Sure",he replied, looking victorious.

"I will be helping the other guys set up the old man's tent over by the tree",said Saleem silently, notifying his parents where he would be.

When Ahmed went back near the tent where he had found Ali, he did not expect to see him sitting outside with a football on his lap.

"You're here",Ali shouted happily, getting up.

"Were you sitting outside the whole time?",asked Ahmed.

"No",lied the boy. "I just came out,do you want to go play?"

"Sure", smiled Ahmed, following Ali to a clearing where other kids were playing all sorts of games, for a moment, Ahmed felt like a normal child. A child who was getting to spend his childhood doing things that an actual kid does. But it didn't last very long, because a few minutes later, they heard a noise and they looked up. Their eyes widened in fear as they saw what was approaching them from high up above, at neck breaking speed. Oh yes. Another rocket.

CHAPTER ELEVEN

ROCKETS

The rocket falling from the sky came as a shock to all of them. One moment, they were playing. The next, the air was filled with a terrible whistling sound. They barely had time to react before the explosion rocked the earth beneath their feet. Dust and debris filled the air, obscuring their vision.

Ahmed's ears were ringing. And then everything was silent. He could see people screaming, he could see them move, covered in dust and blood. He could see all of it but he couldn't hear anything. He screamed too. But he couldn't even hear his own scream. He started crying, alone and helpless, looking for Ali who was with him, just moments ago. Ahmed ran around, seeing people pick each other up from the ground. The tents, destroyed. The camp where they had come to seek refuge, gone. In the blink of an eye.

"Mama! Baba!",shrieked Ahmed, even though he couldn't hear his own voice.

He tried running towards their tent but he couldn't spot it. Fires raged, unchecked and the screams of the wounded people filled the air. Slowly, Ahmed was starting to hear things, he could hear those screams and cries. When his hearing slowly returned he wasn't sure if he really wanted it back, because the yells and cries were heartwrenching.

"Mama!",he shouted again and broke down. When he wiped his tears, he saw that he was covered with dust and his hand was bleeding badly. That made him panic even more.

The shock of the rocket was so bad that he hadn't even felt the pain of the wound until his eyes saw it.
He looked around and saw Ali, sitting on the ground, a little far away from him and immediately ran towards the first friendly face he saw, before he could lose it.
"Ali!", Ahmed shouted. "Ali!", he shouted again, while running towards him. He didn't seem to hear him. And Ahmed did not blame him, given the strepitous environment.

When he finally reached Ali, he noticed that Ali had no wounds, except for a scratch on his forehead, probably by some stray missile part. Then Ahmed noticed that there was a body lying down next to where he was sitting. The body of a woman, whose face was half burned and one of her legs was missing. To Ahmed, it seemed that her tent might have gotten right in the way of whoever was aiming those missiles.
Ahmed's first instinct was to get away from the body. But he daringly opened his mouth to ask,"Who is that?".

Already dreading the answer, Ahmed heard a weak "My sister", from Ali. He didn't even see his lips move.
"*inna lillahi wa inna ilayhi raji'un*", whispered Ahmed.
(Translation: Indeed, to Allah we belong and to Allah we

shall return)

Ali repeated the same thing and looked at Ahmed. "What am I going to do now?"

Ahmed had no reply to that.

"She was the only family I had left",Ali mumbled. "What am I going to do without her?"

"You still have me",said Ahmed, seeing a stray tear falling from his friend's eye. "Come with me. We will find my parents and you can come with us wherever we go"

Ali shook his head. "No. I want to stay with her"

He then hugged the body of his sister, whose lifeless eyes were staring up at the sky, and started crying uncontrollably. Ahmed had almost forgotten about his wound for some time. And then a searing pain blinded him. It was coming from his damaged arm. His immediate thought was to run to his Mama but there were no Mama around to fix his arm.

CHAPTER TWELVE

ONLY FAMILY

Ahmed made the decision to leave his sobbing friend there and look for his parents. It seemed like the right move. He had to get his arm healed, it hurt so badly that he kept biting down on his lips. It almost made him wish that he had no arms in the first place.

'Would having no arms be better than having a wounded arm that hurts so bad?',wondered Ahmed, in his tiny little head, as he looked around for his parents.

A hoard of thoughts came to his head. 'Did Ali's sister suffer from the same pain before she finally died? Did she cry when she saw that her leg had been separated from her body? Am I going to die like her, because of this wound, too?'

So many questions, but no one to answer them for him. And finally, Ahmed's eyes landed on a boy wearing a light blue T-shirt.

"Saleem!",he shouted, desparately wanting him to hear his shouts, because he felt like he was going to faint right then and there."Saleem! I am here!"

Fortunately for him, Saleem looked and a wave of relief passed over his face. He came running towards him.
"*Alhamdulillah* (Thank God), I found you",said Saleem as he approached Ahmed. "Mama and Baba were so worried"

Saleem took one look at Ahmed's bleeding arm and then looked back at his brother's face to see if he was scared.

"Dont worry",said Saleem. "It will be alright. We will get it fixed"
That was the exact thing Baba had said to Fatima. But she had died on the operating table. The thought made Ahmed shiver. Would he meet the same fate?
Saleem picked him up and carried him back to a tent where his parents were waiting, with other people.
The reaction of Maryam upon seeing her son's wound wasn't nearly as calm as Saleem. But soon Mahmood calmed her down, comforting her that they would take him to the hospital.

Mahmoud had gotten himself a small truck, and when Ahmed inquired his father about it, his response was a simple "I borrowed it".
As soon as they were about to get inside the car, Ahmed remembered about his friend and instantly said his name,"Ali. He's alone"
"Who?",asked Mahmoud.
"Ali, my friend", repeated Ahmed."His sister died"
"*Inna lillahi wa inna ilayhi raji'un*"
"We have to help him Baba",said Ahmed, looking pale because of losing a considerable amount of blood, but Maryam had wrapped a cloth around it, hoping it would

help.

When they made their way to Ali, he was lying down beside his sister's body. The sight made Maryam tear up again but Mahmoud took charge and approached the young boy.

"You should get up Ali", whispered the Mahmoud ,trying to gently yank him away from his sister's lifeless body, but Ali held on to her even harder.

More tears fell from Ali's eyes and he hugged his sister again.

"You have to let go, Ali", he whispered. "We will give her a proper *Janazah* (burial). Let go"

But Ali was most definitely not letting go of the only family member he had left. It didn't matter to him that she was not alive. It didn't matter that he could no longer feel her warmth. He just wanted to hold on to her a little bit longer. He just wanted to curl up beside her and have her tell him a story. She always told him a story before bedtime. It used to be his mother's job but her sister was good at it too. Ali cried even more, thinking about the future and as to who would take up the mantle of being the storyteller, now. Who would cook for him? Who would make sure that he ate on time? Even when she was hungry herself. Who was going to care for him?

When no answer came to Ali's mind, he closed his eyes and whispered to his sister,"I can't live without you *ukht*. Please take me with you. Ya Allah, I do not want to live anymore."

Mahmoud closed his eyes and strengthened his grip around Ali's shoulder and took him into his arms.

"NOOO!",yelled Ali, trying to go back and hug the body. "My sister!"

"She's gone, son. You are alive. She wouldn't want you to be wishing for your own death",said Mahmoud, kneeling down and comforting him."She's safe now. She'd want you to be safe too."

"I want my sister",cried Ali, his face shining with tears, he hugged Mahmoud, wrapping his arms around his neck. "She was my only family."

Mahmoud hugged him back but didn't say anything this time. He knew he had to take this child with him now.

CHAPTER THIRTEEN

NOT A SAFE AREA

They had buried Ali's sister and had gotten Ahmed patched up. When the doctors were fixing his arm, Ahmed cried the whole time because it felt like his arm was on fire. Before they left the camp, Ali made sure that he got his football back, which they were able to recover easily. Afterall, the football meant a lot to Ali. Ahmed didn't understand why Ali was so attached to the ball. They were on the road now, but Ahmed couldn't figure out where they were going. Saleem sat in the front with his father while Ahmed and Ali sat in the back with Maryam, who was holding on to the baby. Ali held on to his football as though it was the only thing keeping him alive. He wasn't willing to talk yet. Whenever he was asked a question, he either replied with a nod or a shake of his head. Questions that required more than a yes or no, went unanswered.

The once beautiful Gaza city now looked like someone had set it ablaze. Afterall, someone had. Maybe not as much a particular someone than quite culpable, brazen and shamelessly corrupted many.

They hadn't gotten that far when something caught Mahmoud's eyes, resulting in him stopping the truck. An old man was sitting outside a half-destroyed house. The house looked like it was pretty, even though it was almost demolished . The man was just sitting outside, near the half-open door, staring up at the sky. His body was frail and hunched, his clothes threadbare and worn. It seemed as though he had gone through a lot of hardship and heartbreak in his many long years.

"Should we help him, Mahmoud?",asked Maryam, looking at the man too. "It looks like he has no way of getting out of here"

"I'll go ask",replied Mahmoud, getting out of the car. Before Maryam could say anything, Ahmed got out of the car too and followed his father.

"*Assalam o alaikum* (peace be upon you)", said Mahmoud, approaching the old man.

"*Walekum assalam* (and upon you be peace)",replied the old man, with a smile. For a moment, the hard lines on his face softened. His rheumy eyes grew wistful and faraway.

"Can we help you brother?",asked Mahmoud.

"Only *Allah* can",replied the old man.

"What if he sent me to help you?", asked Mahmoud.

The old man smiled and said,"I don't need any help right now."

"This area is not safe, brother. You can come with us. Bombs could fall on you any minute. There is space in my truck, we will get you somewhere safe."

"But I don't want to go anywhere",replied the old man with a smile. "I am just waiting for my death to come"

CHAPTER FOURTEEN

YA HAYATI

"You shouldn't talk like that brother.",said Mahmoud. "You're still alive. Let me help you while I can. You will die if you stay here"

"I know I will die.",said the old guy. "That's why I am here. You see this house? I built it for my wife, thirty two years ago."

"Your wife? She's here too?",asked Mahmoud, gesturing towards the half-destroyed house.

"No, no one's in there. She's here", the old man pointed at a spot beside the house, which looked like a grave. "She was my life. Ya Hayati, Ya Rohi" (My Life, My Soulmate)

Now Ahmed noticed the shovel lying down beside the grave. Ahmed had dug a grave with his father and brother before. He knew how hard it was. The digging part wasn't nearly as hard as the part where you buried your loved one. Ahmed couldn't imagine doing it alone. But this old man had done it all by himself.

"Wouldn't your wife want you to save yourself?",asked Mahmoud.

"It doesn't matter. She's not here anymore",said the old man, in a low voice. A profound sadness lurked in his eyes."I loved her so much. But they killed her. They killed her. I built this house for her. We used to live here and they destroyed it."

Mahmoud didn't respond, he went ahead and sat down next to the man.

"So your plan is to die here?",asked Mahmoud.

"No",replied the man, "I'm just ready, for when death comes, I'll gladly embrace it."

"When did you last eat?",asked Mahmoud

"Yesterday"

"Come with us, get in truck. There's space in the back of the truck, you can take some things with you, if you like",said Mahmoud, getting up.

"Everything I like is already here, son. You go ahead, you have a lot to live for",said the man looking up at Mahmoud and gesturing towards the truck filled with his family and his son, Ahmed standing behind him.

Mahmoud took a deep breath and said in a relatively low voice,"I'm asking you for the last time"

"You go ahead with your family son",said the man."I'll stay here and guide the people who show up here as to where the safe area is."

Mahmoud dejectedly walked back to the truck and Ahmed followed him. Right before getting inside the truck, Ahmed spared one last look at the old man and realised he looked at peace with his decision. Tranquil, even. Ahmed couldn't imagine how lonely the man must be feeling. No *Mama*, no *Baba*, no siblings and a recently deceased wife. How does one live after that? And then Ahmed realised, he wasn't really living. The man was waiting for his death. No one should have to go through that. When Ahmed turned back and got inside the car, he had tears in his eyes but he quickly wiped it away.

CHAPTER FIFTEEN

A BRILLIANT IDEA

There were tents by the side of a hospital and Mahmoud had instructed Ali, Ahmed and Maryam to stay inside with their baby, while he and Saleem went around and helped the injured get to the hospital or make themselves useful in some way. Ahmed didn't like staying there. The coppery smell of blood was too overpowering, but Maryam had consoled him with "we won't be staying here for long, they'll be back with food soon."

Ahmed was bored but he was not allowed to go out and he didn't even want to. When he went out he saw people with chopped off limbs, mothers holding their dead children and young men and women crying, holding the bodies of their dead parents or spouses. Ahmed looked at Ali, who was still sitting in the corner of the tent, holding on to his football.

"You want to play?",asked Ahmed, pointing at the football.

"We are not allowed to go out",said Ali.

"We can play here",said Ahmed, sitting down on the ground. "We'll play catch."

The place was really small, but they made the best of it. It could barely be called a game of catch, but it definitely made Ali feel a little better. He smiled every time Ahmed missed a catch or if he missed one. You'd have to be really bad at it to be missing a catch that is being thrown from such a small distance. Maryam watched them play and smiled to finally be able to see children doing things that they should be doing instead of worrying about being alive.

Maryam put Halima down next to her, she yawned and proceeded to lay down next to her. She opened her mouth and instructed Ali and Ahmed before dozing off,"Whatever happens, you two will not go outside. Stay here until your father or Saleem comes back with supplies"

For some time, they behaved like good kids and continued playing catch, but soon they got bored of it and Ahmed had a brilliant idea.

"You want to go outside, Ali?",asked Ahmed, his eyes shining with wild curiosity.

"But your Mama will get angry. She has told us to stay here"

"We'll be back before she knows it",said Ahmed getting up. "Maybe we will be able to help a few people too."

"I am scared though",said Ali, his eyes showing fear. "There's so much death and blood outside"

"But we can act like men. We will be able to rescue people Ali. Dont you want to help someone?",asked Ahmed. "Or don't you atleast want to know what's going on outside?"

Ali finally nodded and got up, putting the ball down, near Maryam's foot and followed Ahmed outside the tent, not knowing they were making an extremely poor decision.

CHAPTER SIXTEEN

SKULLS AND TEARS

First the strong smell of blood hit Ahmed and made him close his eyes for a minute.

"Maybe I shouldn't be out here",he thought, but then immediately looked at Ali and changed his mind. He had to prove to Ali that he knew how to be a man. He had to prove to him that he was just as capable as his older brother and his father. He was equally capable of helping people.

With that thought, he marched ahead. Ali followed him and soon they heard a wailing noise. A woman screaming.

Immediately they ran in that direction and saw a woman standing outside the hospital, with some people gathered around. There were some people wearing blue vests with the words "P-R-E-S-S" printed on them. They were carrying cameras and small mics. Ahmed wondered if they were the same people he used to see on television when his Baba would change the channel from cartoon to news. Were the cameras capturing these moments? Would they be shown off on someone's Television too? Ahmed had many questions on his mind. But the most important one was why that woman was screaming. He scanned her fully and she didn't look very hurt. She was standing, but she kept screaming and waving a piece of small red toy, looking at the camera of a man in vest who was recording it.

Ahmed started paying close attention to what the woman was actually saying.

"THIS IS ALL THAT IS LEFT OF HIM! THIS IS WHAT IS LEFT OF MY CHILD! ARE YOU HAPPY NOW? IS THIS WHAT I'M SUPPOSED TO LIVE WITH? MY SON DID NOT DESERVE IT! NO ONE DESERVES THIS!",screamed the woman, looking directly into the camera, tears falling from her eyes.

New questions bloomed inside Ahmed's mind. Were the people responsible for this cruel treatment, on the other side of the camera? Would they be able to see them? Will they finally realise what pain they are causing? Maybe this will make them stop, right? And then with horror, Ahmed looked at the thing that woman was holding. It was no small red toy. It was a piece of her son's body. Ahmed couldn't figure what piece it was, but as if the woman heard him, she shouted at the camera again.

"ALL THAT I HAVE LEFT OF HIM IS HIS PIECE OF SKULL. WHAT DO I DO WITH THIS? HE DIED HUNGRY! HE HAD NO FOOD IN HIS STOMACH! HE WAS WOUNDED TOO AND THEN HE WAS BLOWN TO SMITHEREENS! IMAGINE IF THIS WAS YOUR CHILD"

Ahmed immediately passed a hand through his head, feeling his skull underneath. It felt hard. It felt intact. He shivered. It was unimaginable. Ahmed staggered for a moment but then got a hold of himself. He had to keep moving. Ali was standing silently beside him, with tears in his eyes.

"Dying is better than this",he said in a low voice, tears shining in his eyes.

"Dont say that",Ahmed wanted to say, but he felt Ali was right. What was happening? If the ultimate goal is for all of them to be killed, then what was the point of striving to survive?

"We should go ahead, we should see if someone else needs our help.",said Ahmed, walking to the other side of the road and leaving behind the crying, heartbroken mother who had just lost a son but was either extremely fortunate or exceedingly hapless because atleast she managed to salvage a part of her son's skull. Right?

CHAPTER SEVENTEEN

PIECES

When Ahmed's eyes fell on a man, with a long beard looking through rubble, he decided to go and offer his help, because he thought someone must be stuck underneath and Ahmed considered himself to be pretty strong so he could help the man move through the rubble and Ali followed Ahmed silently.

The man didn't look very sad, or heartbroken. He looked fine to Ahmed.

"Maybe he lost something in the rubble", thought Ahmed. It would be easy to help him. They would just have to rummage through all the ruins.

"Can we help you uncle?",asked Ahmed, walking up to the man.

The man gave Ahmed a big smile and said,"I'm afraid not, child. I was just looking for something."

"Maybe we can help you find it",said Ahmed, pointing at Ali and himself. "We're stronger than we look. We can lift these pieces"

The man chuckled and said,"I'm sure you're very strong. Where are your parents?"

"My Mama is asleep back in the tent and Baba is out looking for food and helping people with Saleem"

"Who's Saleem?"

"My older brother",smiled Ahmed.

"And how did that happen?",asked the man, pointing at Ahmed's bandaged arm.

"We were in tents and bombs came out of nowhere. We barely made it out. But I got this wound",said Ahmed proudly, lifting his arm. Then he looked back at Ali and continued,"His sister died in the bombing."

The man whispered the same prayer under his breath and looked at Ahmed,"Is he not your brother?"

"No, he's my friend. His whole family is dead. He is staying with us",said Ahmed.

Ali was quiet the whole time and the man noticed it.

"Do you not speak child?",asked the man looking at Ali and smiling.

Ali nodded.

"What is your name?",asked the man

"Ali",he said in a loud enough voice.

"It will be fine, Ali. You understand me? Don't be so sad. Your family is in a better place now. Everything will be fine, *Inshallah*. My son's name was Ali too, you know"

"Where is he?", prompted Ahmed.

"Oh he died yesterday",said the man, touching is beard. "He was killed by a bomb, just like his sister"

The man waited around for a minute and then continued looking through the rubble again.

"What are you looking for?",asked Ali, trying to make conversation with the man.

"I.....I-uh....I am looking for my son",said the man.

"Ali?"

"Yes", replied the man, moving a big piece of rubble.

"But you just said he died",said Ahmed, frowning.

"Yes, he died. I am collecting his pieces.",said the man, looking back at the two boys.

"P-pieces?", whispered Ali.

And then their eyes found the small white plastic bag beside the man. Something that they had not noticed earlier. The plastic bag which was originally white, was stained with blood and a foot was sticking out of it. A severed foot. Some other pieces of his son's body was in the plastic bag too, but Ahmed quickly looked away. His heart was racing fast. He didn't feel so good all of a sudden.

Was it a human foot in a plastic bag that he had just laid his eyes upon? It couldn't be. How strong did a man need to be in order to be collecting his own dead son's severed pieces.

"Why....why are you collecting it?",asked Ahmed.

"It would be disrespectful to leave it lying around.", responded the man. "I want to give my only son a proper burial."

"This is what a man is.", thought Ahmed. "I can never be a man. I can never be this strong."

And Ahmed turned around to trace his steps back to his tent and Ali followed.

CHAPTER EIGHTEEN

HUNGER

When Ahmed made his way back to the tent, Ali followed him and kept asking him why they were going back without helping anyone. Ahmed said he wasn't feeling well but he knew he couldn't help anyone without puking. The smell of blood made him dizzy. The sight of severed body pieces made his throat close up. How would he be capable of helping injured people when he couldn't stand to look at them for more than a few seconds.

He found the tent without any problems and found his mother and his little sister, still asleep.

"Are you hungry?",asked Ahmed and Ali nodded in reply.

"Should we wake her up and tell her that?"

"I don't think so",said Ali. "We should let her sleep. Your father and Saleem will be back soon, right?"

They decided to lie down next to Ahmed's mother when Saleem entered with a bag.

"We found some vegetables",he announced keeping the bag down. "Is Mama still asleep?"

Ahmed nodded and Saleem put a finger to his lips indicating him to be quiet.

"Let her sleep",Saleem mouthed.

Ahmed didn't want to disturb his mother but he was also quite hungry and his mother was the only one capable of cooking up something for them to eat.

"Where's Baba?",asked Ahmed, trying to take his mind away from the vegetable bag on the ground.

"He's helping people get to the hospital in his truck",said Saleem.

Maryam woke up soon enough, and Ahmed started wondering if it was because of his sheer telepathy that he was trying to convey to his mother, telling her how hungry he was. He felt shy claiming it out loud because there were people dying of hunger and he didn't want to sound ungrateful because indeed he had more than half the people around him.

CHAPTER NINETEEN

UNDER A BUILDING

Things were falling apart. Ahmed was frantically screaming for his Mama. Bombs had fallen on the hospital again and Mahmoud was trying to get Ali, Ahmed, Salim, Maryam and the infant safely to the truck so that he could drive them to a place safer than this. Unfortunately, Ahmed had gotten separated from the group and he went inside the building again, so that he could be safe there until his parents found him, which was a big mistake as it was on the verge of falling, and it did.

Ahmed had never experienced what being in an extremely small space felt like. He didn't even know he was claustrophobic until now. His arm was stuck under a lot of rubble and he could see light at the far end. He knew he could crawl there if his hand wasnt stuck. He was panicking and he had already tried screaming for help. He just felt more thirsty so he stopped himself from shouting any further but his heart was pacing very fast.

Trapped beneath the weight of a collapsed building, his hand pinned beneath the debris, Ahmed tried to stay conscious and alert, his survival instincts kicking in as he tried to remain calm amidst the chaos surrounding him. As he struggled to free his hand, Ahmed's mind raced with thoughts of his family and Ali wondering if they were safe and if they knew that he was trapped.

The dust and rubble obscured his vision, but he could hear distant voices calling out for help, giving him hope that rescue was on the way. But it still didn't arrive. Ahmed kept hoping that he'd hear someone calling out his name and he'd shout back in response. One of Ahmed's hand was already injured from the camp and now the other hand didn't look so good too. Ahmed shuddered at the thought of losing his hands.

He remembered the time he was in the hospital the night Fatima died. He remembered seeing a man holding two small decapitated hands and he remembered being scared and cowering behind his parents.

A disturbing image formed in Ahmed's head of Mahmoud holding Ahmed's decapitated hands, with blood dripping from the ends, just like the man in the hospital was. The thought made him so scared that he started crying.

"*Ya Allah*, save me from this and I will pray *Salah Al-Shukr* (prayer of thankfulness)", cried Ahmed, once again trying to pull his hand out.

Around an hour had passed and still no one had rescued him. He was starting to feel a little dizzy now. He kept wiping the sweat off his face with his little hand. He was starting to realise how parched he was.

"Hey",came a voice from infront which startled Ahmed. He looked around in the darkness and saw a man looking at him. He was stuck under the rubble too, but his arms were free and he could easily crawl to the distant hole but Ahmed was the obstacle between the man and the small rupture in the rubble that led outside. Ahmed wondered how long the man had been lying there or if he'd just crawled up to him from far off.

"Help me", whispered Ahmed immediately.

"Help is on the way", replied the man in a beautiful voice. He smelled very nice too for someone stuck under a collapsed building. The man stretched out his hand and handed Ahmed a water bottle, after uncapping it.

"Where did that come from?",asked Ahmed confused.

"You're thirsty, drink it",said the man in a comforting voice.

Ahmed didn't question him any further and immediately drank up the water, leaving a bit of water for the man.

"You are exhausted, why don't you sleep?",asked the man.

"I have to stay awake so that if I see anyone walking by I'll scream for help",said Ahmed, feeling like crying again.. "If I sleep and they shout to check if there is someone under the rubble and I don't reply, they'll go away."

"You sleep, child. I will keep a watch and if I see any movements or hear anyone nearby, I'll shout for help.",said the man.

Ahmed put his head down with his face towards the hole, still unsure if he should close his eyes. Sleeping definitely seemed like a better alternative for crying and panicking. But how could he get himself to sleep under such circumstances. His hand was stuck and his other hand which had been previously injured was starting to throb now.
But surprisingly, the moment he closed his eyes, he fell asleep.

CHAPTER TWENTY

RESCUE

Ahmed woke up to someone shining a light in his face. He opened his eyes and tried to bring his hands to cover his face and then realised one of his hands was stuck under the rubble.

"Oh right",Ahmed remembered. "It wasn't a dream afterall"

"Is someone there?",came the voice of a man.

"Yes! Yes! I am here. I am alive! Help me!",shouted Ahmed.

"Can you crawl up here son?", asked the man.

"No!",shouted Ahmed. "My hand. It is stuck. I can't move it"

"Is there someone else in there with you?",asked the man.

Ahmed turned around to look at the man who had given him water before he had dozed off, but there was no one there. There was space that led to the other side, but Ahmed knew that the kind man wasn't thin enough to fit through there. Where did he go?

"There was a man in here with me",said Ahmed. "He is not here anymore. Did he get out?"

"I don't think so, son. We just got to this side of the building, we haven't taken anyone out from here yet."

"But he was right here",said Ahmed.

"Okay, stay in there. We will try to get you out.",said the man walking away to the other side.

"Please don't leave!",yelled Ahmed. "Please don't leave uncle."

"I am not leaving son. I will just go and get a few men here, to help me move all this and get you out. I won't leave you here", promised the man.

This gave Ahmed some comfort. The man wouldn't leave Ahmed. He was going to get him out. The question nagging at the back of Ahmed's head was as to where the man who gave him water, went. There was no possible way out, other than the one Ahmed was looking at and to get to that hole, one would have to crawl there but Ahmed was right in the middle, so the man couldn't have possibly been able to reach the hole to escape.

After another painfully long hour, the brave men had managed to make the hole in the rubble, bigger. It was big enough to fit a man who then crawled inside, helped Ahmed free his hand and then crawled back out with Ahmed. The building could have collapsed on top of them again, but the men didn't care, they knew that such a death would just take them to *jannah* (paradise).

When Ahmed was finally out, he looked at his hand and found them to be purple and oddly disfigured, there was a long cut on his index finger too, and that was the only finger he could move and feel.

"There was a man in there with me",said Ahmed, looking at the men who had just saved him.

"We checked the whole area, there is no one here anymore",said one of the men, which made Ahmed question his own mind.

CHAPTER TWENTY-ONE

JUST A CHILD

Then his attention went to his hand, which wasn't obeying Ahmed's nerve impulse.

"I can't feel all of my hand",said Ahmed, tears welling up in his eyes. The palm was hurting a lot.

"It was crushed",said a man, wearing green scrubs. "We have to amputate the arm"

"W-what",said Ahmed, his heart pounding.

"We have to amputate your arm",said the man. "I am a doctor, your hand needs to be separated from your body"

"Separated?"

"We need to cut it off"

"No!", screamed Ahmed. "You can't do that!"

"Son, listen to me",said the doctor approaching Ahmed. Ahmed kept backing up. "If we don't cut it off now, it will cause problems."

"I want Mama",cried Ahmed. "Mama and Baba will know what to do"

"Were they in this building with you?",asked a man.

"No",replied Ahmed. "Baba was taking us to his truck so he could drive us out of here because bombs were falling. But I got separated so I came inside the building because it was crowded outside. I came inside so they could find me easily but the building fell."

"What are their names? And what's your name?"

"Mahmoud Qaradawi and Maryam Ubaid",replied Ahmed. "I am Ahmed Qaradawi"

"Okay Ahmed. We'll find them. But until then, you come with us and we will do something about that arm, okay?"

"No, don't cut it off, please",said Ahmed, down on his knees, begging. "I like to paint. I like to draw. I won't be able to play marbles or play catch. Please let me keep my hand"

The men looked at each other woefully.

"Ahmed, if I don't amputate your hand now, you won't be able to keep your full arm in some time. We don't have the facility to treat it. We have to cut it."

"Please",said Ahmed, tears blinding his eyes. "I'm just a child. I can't live without my hand"

A man went ahead and picked up Ahmed in his arms and Ahmed did not resist. He put a hand on Ahmed's back, comforting him and said,"It will be fine. A child who lives through all this isn't a child anymore. You're a man now. Be brave and *Allah* will make it easier for you."

Ahmed did not respond to any of that. He kept weeping, without being able to wipe his own tears. All of the adrenaline had faded, now he could feel the throbbing pain being sent up his arm and to his shoulders.

"It's hurting a lot", Ahmed turned and said to the doctor.

"Come with me",said the doctor leading the men to a small house. "I have some equipments at my home."

"We are not going to the hospital?",asked Ahmed

"What do you think you were stuck under the ruins of?",asked the man carrying him.

CHAPTER TWENTY-TWO

NO ANAESTHESIA

They entered the doctor's house who proceeded to clear out his kitchen table. He took out a bag from his cupboard and started taking out equipments from it. Ahmed saw some very sharp instruments which made him dizzy.

Ahmed felt nauseous,"I think I'm gonna--"

And he puked.

"I- I'm scared", admitted Ahmed, starting to cry.

"You're about to lose a limb here",said the doctor. "I'd be more concerned if you weren't scared"

"I need Mama",said Ahmed. "Someone please find her."

"I promise Ahmed, we will find your family right after this is done. Just trust Allah, son. It will be alright.",said the man who was carrying him. "I will be right here."

"We don't have any anaesthesia, Ahmed. So you will feel the pain it causes",said the doctor

"Okay, okay. Do it",said Ahmed, his heart beating faster than ever.

"Do you know any *surahs*?",asked the man

"Yes. I know *Surah Al-Fatiha*", replied Ahmed.

"Recite it. Loudly."

Ahmed obeyed while he was put down on the table and the doctor assessed the damage and started getting to work.

When it was all done, Ahmed could barely open his eyes. He had them shut tight through the whole procedure.
He had started screaming once the doctor cut into his skin but the man held his other hand and told him to keep remembering Allah and to keep reciting the *Surah*. Ahmed felt the pain, but it was a dimmed down version of the pain. During the procedure he dared to open his eyes once and the sight of so much blood made him close them again. He could feel everything that was being done to his arm. He heard the roar of the machine that was going to separate his arm and the sound made him so scared that he called out for his Mama and his Baba but neither of them could hear him. So he called out to someone who he knew was listening, *Allah*.

When it was all done, Ahmed looked at his hands. It was fully bandaged and had been amputated. There was no hand anymore, just his arm extending to just a little bit more than his elbow.

"You were so brave son",said the man.

Ahmed tried to sit up but he felt dizzy and lied back down.

"You lost a lot of blood",said the doctor. "Rest for a while, I'll get something for you to eat."

Ahmed overheard the men talking about looking for an IV drip for him and then he fell asleep.

CHAPTER TWENTY-THREE

WHEN HE WILLS

At first Ahmed thought he was dreaming when he saw his mother sitting infront of him with Halima in her arms and his Baba, Ali and Salim standing beside her.

"Mama?", croaked Ahmed opening his eyes fully.

Maryam got up, handed Halima to Mahmoud and immediately hugged Ahmed.

"I'm so sorry we lost you", said Maryam, sobbing.

"Mama, I lost an arm.",said Ahmed breaking down. "I- I lost my arm."

"It's okay Ahmed.", said his mother. "It was *Allah's* will. Don't cry."

She then wiped his tears and quoted a verse in the Qur'an, "Remember son, *Inna ma'al 'usri yusra*" (indeed with hardship comes ease).

"When will this end Mama?",asked Ahmed crying with his face buried in his mother's stomach. "When can we go back to our home?"

"When *Allah* wills",she said.

They exited the house and Mahmoud led the way as they traced the path back to the truck. Ahmed turned his head to look around, only to see destruction everywhere. Ruins covering the streets. Roads painted red with blood. People with injuries that made Ahmed flinch before looking at them.

Ahmed had eaten whatever his parents had salvaged and sitting in the backseat of the car, looking at everything with one less hand attached to his body didn't make him feel any different. Ahmed doubted if he'd feel the same when someone asked him to play marbles with him or hold a bat while playing cricket. Would he be able to balance himself while playing football? Would he ever be able to play catch again? All the thoughts were piling up in his head. No answers yet again. Just the wind blowing against his face.

Ahmed's mind travelled to the man under the rubble who had offered him water. Who was he? Where did he go? Why was everything so confusing these days?
Ahmed knew that tomorrow is never promised but with everything happening, it just made it more certain.

Ahmed put his head on his mother's arm and closed his eyes. She held him ever so lightly. She caressed his cheek and put a hand on his forehead and started massaging which led him to immediately fall into a deep sleep.

CHAPTER TWENTY-FOUR

VULTURES

Falling. Falling away. He tried to get ahold of something but he kept falling without anything nearby to hold on to. He tried to scream but he couldn't. He finally hit the ground, but he wasn't hurt, not even little bit. He got up and looked around to better evaluate the place he'd just fallen in and he saw bodies lying on the ground. Ahmed saw dead bodies as far as his eyes could see, in all directions. He knelt down and his eyes searched for his parents, Saleem, Halima and Ali. Soon, he found them, lying on the ground. Dead.
Ahmed put a hand on his mother's face and whispered,"You promised you would never leave"

He looked at their lifeless bodies and saw vultures gathering around to feast on their bodies. Their sharp beaks made him wince and he looked around for help. But he knew there was no help coming.

"They are my family. Please find something else to eat",said Ahmed, as nicely as he could.

One of the vultures opened its beak only to say something in Saleem's voice,"Come on, wake up Ahmed."

Ahmed woke up, apprehensive, his heart beating very fast.

"Were you having a bad dream?",asked Saleem

Ahmed nodded.

"Don't worry, we're here. You're safe now.",said Saleem."But you have to eat now, you've been asleep for eleven hours"

"Where are we?",asked Ahmed.

They weren't in the car anymore, they were in a house and Ahmed was sleeping on the bed.

"This is the house of a friend of Baba's. He said it is safe for the time being. Come on, let's go, they are waiting for us.",said Saleem, leading the way."It was real arduous work getting the food. The line was so long and the food was about to be finished but we were just on time. We shared ours with the people at the back of the line too, who didn't get the food."

Ahmed kept nodding but he was really disturbed. He had lost an arm. Then he'd had a dream about losing his entire family in one go.

Ahmed reached the table and greeted the man who greeted him back and they all sat down to dine together with a *Bismillah*. Ahmed looked around and saw his family but the man who was a friend of his Baba, didn't have any family. He was alone there.

"Do you live here alone uncle?", Ahmed blurted out.

The muscles in the man's jaw tightened.

"Now, yes. I used to live here with my wife and three kids. They all were murdered."

Ahmed whispered a prayer and looked down at his plate. How horrible must it be to live all alone.

'Is it scarier to die first? Or is scarier to be the one to see your loved ones go first?',wondered Ahmed.

Ahmed didn't want anything more than to sit there with his family and for everything to go back to normal. He didn't want anything else. He was even willing to trade his good pair of pants back at home, with whoever was bombing them in exchange for them to stop all of it. But it never seemed to stop. It just kept getting worse. And here Ahmed ruminated at how silly he was being when he thought that nothing could be worse than his teachers at school.

CHAPTER TWENTY-FIVE

PRESS

Ahmed had gone out with Ali and Saleem.

He looked around and saw a crowd of children around a man wearing a blue vest with the letters P-R-E-S-S printed on it.

"Press?", mouthed Ahmed, wondering what it actually meant. The man was carrying a mic and there was another man carrying a camera who was going around filming them. The man with the vest was talking to the children while the other man filmed them.

Ahmed immediately felt a surge of energy. Would he be seen by the people who were reason behind all this chaos? Would be able to plead to them to stop? Ahmed held Ali's hand and ran towards the man.

The man acknowledged him with a smile as he was talking to another girl

"What do you want the most in the world, right now?",asked the man.

"Baba",said the girl.

"Who are you living with, right now?"

"My grandmother",said the girl.

"Where is she?"

"She's very old. She can't get out of bed easily and so the doctor told her to get a lot of bedrest. And I also wish we had something to eat."

"When did you last eat?"

"Yesterday evening Baba came back with food and then he went out again and he was shot and killed"

"You haven't had anything to eat since then?"

The girl nodded her head, but she was still smiling. Ahmed tilted his head wondering why she was smiling when suddenly he saw her eyes filling up with tears. The smile still was not fading. A tear rolled down her cheek and now her smile broke to show despondency on her face. Who knew that such a young face was capable of showing so much pain.

The camera man put the camera down and gestured towards a man who was distributing something to people.

"Get her food and for her grandmother too",said the man.

The girl was told to follow the man.

The camera turned towards Ahmed.

The man with the mic asked him,"What's your name, son?"

"Ahmed"

"What happened to your arm?"

"I was trapped under a hospital when it was bombed, so the doctors had to cut it off. It doesn't hurt that much though.", smiled Ahmed, putting on a brave face.

"You are a valorous young man",said the reporter patting him on the back. "If there was anything in the world that you could ask for, what would it be?"

It was an intense question. Ahmed had initially planned on asking for people to stop this chaos. To have everything go back to normal. To have everyone smiling and laughing instead of screaming and crying. To get the people incharge to stop bombing them whenever they pleased.

But now, with a camera in his face and a mic to speak his words into, those words failed to come out. Instead a faint whisper came out,"Fatima"

"Who is Fatima?"

"My sister, she died when a building fell on her and the doctors tried to save her but they couldn't", said Ahmed fighting back tears at this point. He didn't want his tears to be recorded. He didn't want the whole world to see him crying. He was still 8 years old but the circumstances were moulding him into someone far older.

When it was Ali's turn to speak, his answer to the question was "my family" which made Ahmed even sadder. Sometimes he failed to remember that Ali had lost his entire family to this madness. Ahmed still shuddered while imagining his whole family dead.

"It was just a dream. It won't actually happen",Ahmed whispered to himself and focused back on Ali who was still talking to the man with the vest.

CHAPTER TWENTY-SIX

BRAVE?

Ahmed had gone out with Saleem, he saw the whole area. He had gotten quite familiar with it now, as Saleem had shown him quite a few places. Ahmed knew he could get used to anything except for the loss of his arm. He just didn't know how to deal with it. How could he go about doing his day-to-day activities without an arm? Yes, his family was helping him but it still didn't help him get over losing it.

"Mama when everything goes back to normal and I go to school, will kids make fun of me?",he had asked his mother last night.

"No Ahmed, ofcourse not. No one is going to make fun of you. If anything, they'll call you brave."

"But....but I'm a child. I'm not supposed to be brave"

"This genocide has made people a lot of things they weren't supposed to be",said his mother.

"Do you think it will ever stop?"

"When *Allah* wills it to stop. It will."

"So, this is another test for us?"

"Not just for us Ahmed. This is a test for the entire *Ummah*",she said slowly stroking his hair.

Saleem's voice zapped Ahmed back to reality.

"Hey Ahmed, look at this",said Saleem pointing at a cat.

"It's so cute. Will Mama let us keep it?",asked Ahmed, grinning for the first time in days.

Before Saleem could answer, they heard a shuffle behind them and turned around to see four men in military overalls with combat gear holding huge guns.

Ahmed's heart skipped a beat.

"What are you kids doing here?", asked a soldier lazily.

And they both understood they had strayed too far away from home.

"We were just going home",said Saleem, avoiding eye contact, grabbing Ahmed by his one arm and turning around to go back.

"HEY! YOU LOOK AT ME WHEN I'M TALKING TO YOU!",said the soldier pushing Saleem hard.

"I said we are going back",said Saleem, his nostrils flaring with pure anger. Ahmed gripped Saleem's hand tightly. He was scared.

"Are you carrying something?",asked another soldier coming forward.

They seemed to be enjoying themselves.

"No", replied Ahmed quickly.

"No one asked you!",the soldier snapped at Ahmed.

"Turn around, let us check if you are carrying something",said the soldier, preparing himself to check Saleem thoroughly to see if he was carrying anything that he was not supposed to be carrying.

The man was inappropriate with his checking and Ahmed opened his mouth again.

"He's not carrying anything!"

"Shut up, you disabled bastard!",a soldier cried at Ahmed.

Those words stung him.

"What did you call my brother?!",Saleem spun around indignantly.

He wanted to hit them but he knew what the consequences of that would be. He would also get overpowered easily because it was 1 against 4.

"Who are you getting angry at, boy?,said the soldier, holding up his gun. "Or did you forget who has the gun here?"

"Guns, in the hands of cowards dont make them superior.",said Saleem gritting his teeth.

"Did you call us cowards, boy?",said the soldier aiming a gun at Saleem's leg and immediately firing.

CHAPTER TWENTY-SEVEN

HOSPITAL OR GRAVEYARD?

A crimson stain bloomed on Saleem's patched trousers, spreading like a malevolent flower. His calloused hand clutched at his leg, where a bullet had ripped through the flesh, leaving a gaping wound that pulsed with pain.

Ahmed's innocent eyes, once bright with childish curiosity, now stared blankly at Saleem, on the ground, reflecting the shock and disbelief that had frozen him in place. The sound of the gunshot still echoed in his ears, a jarring reminder of his brutal reality. Saleem's face contorted in a silent scream of pain. His eyes had involuntarily emitted tears. Tears of sheer pain.

"Who's superior now, boy?",asked the soldier standing over him with the gun pointed at his chest now.

Through the raw pain, Saleem managed to get the words out, "*Allah*".

Right then and there, the man put two in his chest and Saleem's eyes wide with innocence, lay motionless on the ground, bullet wounds gaping red on his chest. The cold-hearted soldier stood over him, his face devoid of any emotion. As Ahmed watched in horror, all he could do was scream his brother's name.

"Saleem!"

He could feel his own heart shatter into a million pieces. Saleem, his older brother, his protector, his playmate, was gone in an instant. The soldier, unfazed by Ahmed's pain, turned and walked away with the other soldiers, their footsteps echoing. Ahmed clung to the hope that Saleem might still be alive, but as he rushed to his side, the cruel reality shattered his hopes.

Saleem's body was cold and lifeless, his gentle smile forever frozen on his face. A wave of unimaginable grief and anger washed over Ahmed as he realized that his beloved brother was gone forever, taken from him by the heartless act of a man who felt no remorse.

"Saleem",he whispered in his brother's ear, tears falling uncontrollably."Saleem, not you too Saleem. Wake up."

Ahmed's hand was shaking. He couldn't figure out what to do. Saleem couldn't be dead. Ahmed refused to accept it.

"Saleem what am I going to tell Mama and Baba? Don't break our hearts. Wake up Saleem. Please brother....please. Don't go away like Fatima",cried Ahmed, his voice breaking just like his heart was. "I'm begging you."

But Saleem did not respond. His eyes kept looking at the sky above.

"Maybe if I take him to the hospital, the doctors will fix him.", thought Ahmed, getting up and looking around.

There was no one around. He couldn't leave his brother's body there alone. So Ahmed tried dragging him. He only had one arm, and the strength of a child. He still managed to pull him for a certain distance, leaving a trail of blood behind them, before he was out of breath.

He looked around for help as his eyes fell on a man.

"Uncle! Uncle! Please help me!",cried Ahmed, glad to have found him. "I need to take my brother to the hospital"

The man's face changed when his eyes fell upon the body Ahmed was dragging. He came close and crouched down beside Saleem's body to inspect if he was still alive and after he was done, he looked at Ahmed and whispered, "Child, we need to take him to a graveyard, not a hospital"

"No no, please don't say that. The doctors can fix him. It's a wound. The doctors cut off my arm to save me and I am fine now. A building fell on my arm and I am fine. It was just two bullets, when the doctors take it out of him, he will be fine.",said Ahmed, with a little confidence now.

"Do you live nearby? Do you have other family members?",asked the man

"Yes, my family is at home. I live that way",said Ahmed pointing his finger at the road they'd taken to come here.

"Okay...I will help you carry him home",said the man, picking up Saleem.

"No please, we don't have time. When Fatima was hurt, the doctors said that she had lost a lot of blood. Saleem is losing too much blood. We have to take him to the hospital.",said Ahmed, helplessly. His breathing was fast and he kept trying to get his hair out of his face with his hand and because of that, his face was now bloody too.

"Your brother is dead, child. Tell me where you live",said the man, with Saleem in his arms.

Blood dripped down from Saleem's body. The man's clothes were covered in blood too. Ahmed thought that the man was lying. But he didn't have any other choice so he led the way. He knew that once they got home, his Baba would immediately take Saleem to the hospital. Because he refused to believe that his brother was dead.

CHAPTER TWENTY-EIGHT

HATES THE COLD

Baba did infact take Saleem to the hospital. The day they buried Fatima was a blur for Ahmed but this time, things were clearer.

Ahmed remembered the man helping him take Saleem's body home. They carried him to the hospital where they pronounced him dead. Ahmed heard his mother screaming when they were taking her son away to keep him in the freezing room.

"Don't take my son away! NOOO! HE HATES THE COLD. Please. I'm begging you, don't take him away",screamed Maryam clutching desparately at Saleem's shirt.

Silent tears rolled down Mahmoud's face but he didn't scream. Not even a little bit.

"Mahmoud, they are taking our son away! Mahmoud, you know that Saleem doesn't like the cold, Mahmoud. Don't let them take him away",cried Maryam, turning to her husband, amidst her hiccups and tears.

"We will give him a burial, Maryam don't worry",said Mahmoud, kissing on top of Maryam's covered head. "May *Allah* continue taking away from our blood until he be pleased."

All Ahmed did that day, was cry. Two of his siblings dead. Ahmed heard Halima cry too and he wondered whether she was crying because she understood that her brother was dead or if she was just hungry. Most probably the latter, but Ahmed took comfort in the fact that he still had a sister.

Ahmed kept trying to get the image of his brother getting shot, out of his head. The defeaning sound of the bullet leaving the gun. The sound Ahmed heard when the bullet tore his brother's skin. The thud with which Saleem's body fell to the ground. It was all too much for Ahmed's mind to bear. Ahmed wished there was an instrument that could make him forget all of that. Something that could clean his mind of all the things it had seen and stored in the past few days.

He went outside but didn't stray away too far. Ahmed was looking around with his puffy red eyes when his eyes landed on something. A truck. An ice-cream truck! Ahmed smiled despite the pain. He remembered how much he loved ice creams. He still remembered the time when everything was normal and his father would come to pick him up from school and upon hearing the bell of the ice-cream truck, his heart would flutter with joy.

Ahmed scurried towards the ice cream truck. He didn't have any money with him but maybe the owner would let him have one ice cream. The backdoor of the truck was open. For a happy moment, Ahmed forgot everything. He forgot about all the pain, he forgot about having only one hand, he forgot that his beloved siblings had said their goodbyes, he forgot all the pain and all he was looking forward to, was an ice-cream. Ahmed peeked inside and his heart skipped a beat. The ice-cream truck was filled with dead bodies.

CHAPTER TWENTY-NINE

ANOTHER ICE-CREAM TRUCK

There was blood all around inside the ice-cream truck. There was a man standing on the other side of the truck, he noticed a young boy peeking in so he immediately darted to close the door.

"Nothing to see here boy",said the man closing the door of the truck.

Ahmed was silent for a minute and then he found the courage to get these words out of his mouth,"I thought there were ice-creams in here"

"No ice-creams, sorry",said the man comfortingly.

"Why are there bodies here?",asked Ahmed, his eyes still wide from horror.

"We ran out of places to keep the bodies so we are storing whatever bodies we can find, here",said the man looking up at the sky. "Who knows how many more we are going to collect today"

That did not comfort Ahmed. He turned away and ran. Ran away from the ice-cream truck. Ran away from what he had just seen. Ran away from the bodies. Ran away from all things real. He just wished he could run away from here the same way, with his family. He wiped his tears with his arms and cried some more. He would never be able to eat ice-cream again. He would never be able to look at ice-cream trucks the same way, again. Seeing ice-cream trucks and hearing the bell used to elevate his spirits, now it would just be a reminder of what had happened. Now it would just remind Ahmed of all the blood, the bodies and the smell.

Oh, how he wished he could run away and forget everything but he stopped and he changed his wish. He did not wish to go away anymore. His siblings had died in their homeland. They had died in their own land and if Ahmed were to die tomorrow, he would want to be buried beside them. He would want the comfort of dying in his homeland. Now, Ahmed was clear on one thing, that it was HIS homeland and he was NOT leaving. His eyes shone with tears but also with pride for having had that thought.

CHAPTER THIRTY

A MEDICINE

Ali was sitting on the bed while he scribbled some things on a few pieces of paper he had borrowed from the man in whose house they were living, with a pen he had found in the house.

"'Ahmed is not talking to me so much. He hasn't been the same ever since he lost his arm. I don't know what I would do without my arm. I don't have anyone except Ahmed and his parents now. I hope they don't change their minds about me and decide to abandon me all of a sudden. Ahmed doesn't even want to play football with me now. I haven't found a buddy to play football with ever since we left camp. I wish my siblings were here. I wish Ahmed's siblings were here. I wish everything would go back to normal. I wish to see my family alive again but now I will see them in Jannah. My sister always used to tell me that death is not the end and indeed, it is not. Halima keeps crying all the time. We haven't eaten since yesterday. Uncle Mahmoud said we have to go someplace else to find food.'"

They were still going from one place to another. Without any hope of a stable food source. Sometimes they had to go the whole day without eating. Mahmoud was spending his hours searching for food and helping people when he could, but he was not coming back very successful. He was unable to feed his family and that broke him. He somehow felt responsible for the death of Saleem because he was the one who had asked him to go around and see who needed help and that was what Saleem was doing when he was murdered. Mahmoud kept thinking how easily Ahmed could have been killed too.

Maryam had gotten herself together now, because she had to take care of Halima too. She comforted herself by remembering that Salim and Fatima were now in a place where no one could hurt them. They were safe. They were under *Allah's* protection now and soon, she would join them.

They were being hunted by drones now. Shooting at them from the sky. No place was safe for them. They had all been told to go to Rafah, which they claimed to be the safe area.

Ahmed's stomach was hurting due to hunger. He was lying down beside him mother who was nursing Halima.

"Mama?", whispered Ahmed, parting his chapped lips.
"Yes Ahmed?"
"Is there a medicine that *kills* hunger?",asked Ahmed curiously.
"Only food can do that son"
"When I grow up, I will make a medicine that will kill hunger, *Insha Allah*",said Ahmed.

Maryam nodded and slowly patted his head and whispered,"*Insha Allah*". Not because she wanted him to make some pill, but because she wanted him to grow up. She wanted to see him grow up. She wanted to see him have a good life, and live like any other child in the world would.

"Those drones are *not* good, are they?",asked Ahmed. "I saw it shoot some people when we were coming to Rafah."

"No it's not. Don't go near it.",said Maryam, suddenly alarmed.

"Don't worry Mama, I won't",said Ahmed. "When I die, I will tell *Allah* all about this. I will tell him what they are doing to us Mama."

Maryam smiled as his son talked about all the things he was going to tell the *Al-'Aleem* (The All-knowing).

CHAPTER THIRTY-ONE

NO SAFE PLACE

They bombed Rafah too. The only place they were told to go to. The only place they said they wouldn't bomb, they bombed. It was a massacre. Blood everywhere. Ahmed was holding on to Halima with his only hand. Maryam was holding Ali while Mahmoud guided them through the dust.

"They told us to evacuate and go to Rafah, Mama! They said we were safe here!",shrieked Ahmed, panicking at the sight of so many dead bodies around him.

"Ahmed just hold my hand and keep following",said Maryam, coughing and taking Halima in her arms.

Ahmed stumbled, occasionally accidentally stepping on someone. It was impossible not to step on someone's dead body while moving. It felt disrespectful to Ahmed, but he had to keep moving to a safer place with his family.

They finally stopped a bit further, where the dust had settled and the smoke was less.

"Baba, where do we go?",asked Ahmed, panting.

Mahmoud was having a hard time thinking. He was trying to sketch out a plan as to where they should be heading to, next, but his mind was failing him. He fell to his knees, breathing hard.

"Mahmoud! Mahmoud, what happened?!",Maryam ran to his aid.

"I don't know what to do Maryam",said Mahmoud desparately. "I don't know how to keep you all safe anymore. I failed as a father. I couldn't keep Saleem and Fatima safe. They are dead because of me, Maryam. I don't want my entire family to be wiped out!"

Seeing his father so heart broken, so sad, so helpless, Ahmed wept. He had never seen his father so helpless before all this had happened. He always looked up to him as the man who could withstand everything.

"Ssshhhh Mahmoud, look at me! You are the one who always tells me to keep my faith strong. So fight these thoughts. It was not your fault. It was *Allah's* will, Mahmoud. Even if we all die here, we will meet again in Jannah and it will be so much better than the life we could have lived here. Get up Mahmoud, let us fight until we stop breathing. Remember Mahmoud, He does not burden a soul beyond that it can bear.",said Maryam, giving her husband hope.

Mahmoud nodded and he slowly got up and put a hand around Ahmed, who could see his father getting some of the light back in his eyes.

CHAPTER THIRTY-TWO

A DRONE?

It was very sinister. Those drones kept making a buzzing sound, that made Ahmed want to tear his ears out. A continuous buzzing sound, without pausing in between. It was psychological warfare. They were under surveillance at all times. The drones followed them everywhere, could shoot them at any moment. The terror, the constant breath of uncertainty of how there could be a turn of events at any instant, made them all anxious.

Mahmoud told Ahmed that he was going to get in a line to get food for them. He took them to a place where other families were taking shelter too. Mahmoud told them to stay there until he returned. From the moment Mahmoud left, up until the second he returned, Maryam's eyes were darting from one place to another. Mahmoud had got bread and a small box of cooked peas for them. He had also found water. The sight made Ahmed so happy that he almost had tears rolling down his cheeks.

"*Alhamdulillah*",he whispered after hearing his mother do the same. He looked up at the sky with thankful eyes, when he noticed something was off. No drones in sight. They had even stopped making the buzzing noise. It should have been a good thing. Finally not hearing that awful noise anymore. But something felt off. The air was thicker. And then the humming sound began again. It was weird how the humming sound felt normal compared to when there was no sound.

Ahmed turned his head. Was he hallucinating or was the sound actually getting louder? He looked at his parents for confirmation and they looked bewildered too. So he was not hallucinating at all. It was actually getting louder. And they all collectively realised what was happening.

"ITS COMING! EVERYBODY MOVE!", screamed a woman from a little far away. That was enough warning for them. Everyone ran, randomly, in whichever direction they could. Ahmed grabbed a bread before running with his father and Ali. Maryam clutched on to Halima and ran after them.

The drone started firing. They heard a small explosion right where they had just been standing. Ahmed and his family were all hiding inside a building that was half broken. Praying to *Allah* that the drone goes away without coming their way.

The buzzing sound was constant, the drone wasn't going anywhere. And then the sound stopped. They waited for a while.

"Is it gone?", whispered Ali, after some time.

No one had the courage to look up from behind the wall. And that's when they heard it, a baby crying.

Mahmoud's face turned pale, he turned to look at Halima, safely tucked in Maryam's arms and gave out a sigh of relief. But someone's baby was out there. Mahmoud started to get up, but Maryam held him down.

"What do you think you're doing?!", hissed Maryam.

"A child is out there Maryam. If that baby dies, will you be able to live with the guilt knowing we could have saved him. I'll go and come back in a minute. The drone must be round that corner, I'll be back before the drone comes",said Mahmoud pleadingly.

Maryam hesitantly let go of his arm.

Mahmoud went out to save the baby. Ahmed mustered up the courage to look from behind the wall. His eyes went up and he spotted the drone, it wasn't making the buzzing sound anymore. Ahmed looked down, he couldn't spot a baby. And that's when his mind clicked. The sound of the baby crying was coming from the drone.

Before Ahmed could shout,"Baba, it's a trap!", it happened.

The drone fired on his father who had gone out to save a baby that didn't even exist. Ahmed saw it all happen. Maryam heard the shots and her eyes grew wide. Ahmed struggled to get out from behind the wall, to save his father, but Maryam held him down. Tears falling down her cheeks, holding Halima in one hand and a struggling Ahmed in another, she wept.

"Ssssh",said Maryam, her face red and vision blurry.

"Baba", whispered Ahmed, crying. "Baba.....shot"

That's all he could get out of his mouth.

CHAPTER THIRTY-THREE

BROKEN TIES

They waited for some time until Ali confirmed that the drone had gone away. Ahmed ran to his father, hoping he was alive. Hoping, the drone had missed its target and his Baba was just wounded. When they reached Mahmoud, they found him alive, but barely. His breathing was ragged and he was trying to form words with extreme difficultly.

"You said you would come back Mahmoud",cried Maryam, looking at him. "You can't leave me here alone"

"You are not alone", whispered Mahmoud, raising his hand with great difficulty and pointing up at the sky. "He's with you"

"Baba, please. Baba we will call a doctor, please stay for a little while longer. He will know what to do. You have both your arms Baba, see I have one and I am living. Baba please .....",said Ahmed, his voice breaking.

Maryam, sobbing, put a hand over Mahmoud's head and whispered in his ear the shahada,"*Ash-hadu an la ilaha illa Allah, Wa ash-hadu anna Muhammadar Rasulu-Allah*"

(I bear witness that there is no God but Allah and there is none worthy of worship but Allah, and Muhammad is the Messenger of Allah)

Ahmed saw his Baba's lips moving along with Maryam's and he held his father's hand tightly, as he felt the warmth slowly ebbing away. He was struck by the fragility of life, by the fleeting nature of time, and by the inevitability of death. Ahmed was acutely aware of his own mortality, of the fact that one day he too will be facing the end of his journey, just like Fatima, just like Salim and just like his father here.

He got filled with a deep sense of empathy for his Baba, for the pain and suffering he was experiencing, and for the loss that is about to befall them both. The wound looked bad, he was losing too much blood, too fast. No hospitals nearby, Ahmed's mind was racing.

And as his Baba took his last breath, Ahmed was left with a profound sense of loss, but also a profound sense of gratitude to Allah for having had the opportunity to be there for his father in his final moments. In that moment, Ahmed could only hold on tighter, trying to keep his Baba with him for just a little while longer. The weight of the impending loss was almost too much to bear.

As Ahmed looked into his father's eyes, he saw a lifetime of memories flashing before him. The smile his Baba would give him everytime he asked for an ice-cream. The words of wisdom his father would spew on him from time to time. He saw the moments of joy and laughter, of love and support. Ahmed was raw with emotion, feeling the intensity of the bond between them like never before. He knew that his Baba's passing would leave a void in his heart that could never be filled, and that the pain of this loss would be with him always.

The light had vanished from his Baba's eyes, but there was a weird calmness all over his face, as if the body knew how content and at peace the soul was, right now.

The people around, helped them bury Mahmoud's body, because two young boys and a woman with a baby wouldn't have been able to do it on their own.

Ahmed, after a long time, realised he was extremely hungry, but he also felt ashamed asking his mother for food just after they had buried his father. He looked at Ali and he was pretty sure Ali was thinking the same thing. He looked at his mother and she looked lost in thought, as she fed Halima. She noticed Ahmed looking at her and she looked at him with tired, morose eyes.

"I know you're hungry. I will arrange for some food",said Maryam.

"It's fine Mama, me and Ali can go"

"No, you take care of Halima and I will get the food. There is a long line there.", before going, Maryam found them water to sustain themselves with, until she returned.

Ali was holding on to Maryam while Ahmed moved his legs impatiently.

"Why is she not back yet?",asked Ahmed, looking around.

"Ahmed, it has been over 6 hours....I don't think she will be back, we need to go somewhere and search for food ourselves"

"Shut up Ali",retorted back Ahmed. "Mama said she will be back, we have to stay here or she won't be able to find us. The line must be very long"

"The line wasn't that long Ahmed. We both saw it. If she's not back yet, it means something happened to her. Please let's go and find some food ourselves", requested Ali.

"Just because your Mama is dead doesn't mean mine is too!",shouted Ahmed, in anger. "Mama won't just abandon us! She must be searching for food"

Ali was taken aback.

"Why would you say that Ahmed? If you want to die of starvation, then be my guest.",countered Ali.

He put a sleeping Halima in Ahmed's arm, took his ball and walked away.

Ahmed regretted saying that to Ali. He had lost his entire family and yet he had stayed strong and with him from the beginning. Ahmed only had one functioning arm now. There was no way he would be able to survive with Halima alone. He wanted to call out to Ali and beg him not to abandon him, but he had to wait for his Mama to come back. He was convinced that she was not dead. She couldn't be. I mean, who loses their entire family in a span of few weeks.

Ahmed thought to himself,"I can't be that unlucky, right?"

He looked down at Halima, who was sleeping peacefully.

"Mama will come back Halima. I promise", he kissed her forehead and laid back his head on the tree.

CHAPTER THIRTY-FOUR

SEARCH PARTY

Ahmed woke up to Halima crying, it was morning and it was freezing. His stomach rumbled. He was still extremely hungry. Halima had woken up and from the looks of it, she was hungry too. It was morning now and their Mama had still not returned. Ahmed couldn't let the thought, that his mother was dead, into his head. He wanted to cry into someone's arms right now. But whose?

He felt like someone was squeezing his heart. He wasn't able to make a clear sense out of anything at that point. It felt futile. His mother had disappeared. Halima was crying. Ali had left him and everyone else had been murdered. He was all alone, left with a baby to care for. He didn't even know how to take care of himself, how was he going to care for a baby who couldn't even speak when she's hungry or when she wants to sleep.

"Mama", whispered Ahmed, wiping his tears. "Mama, where are you?".

Ahmed was trying to get up when he saw someone approaching them, he couldn't make out their face because he was too exhausted and food-deprived.

"Mama",said Ahmed with a growing smile. But the person was too small to be his Mama. "Ali?"

Ali looked down at him and sat down beside him. He put down his ball and took Halima from his lap, where Ahmed didn't resist and then he handed him some bread and a bottle of water. Ahmed was immediately overtaken by the urge to eat it that very second and he began by drinking the water first and then chomping down big bites off the bread. His mouth was dry so he needed the assistance of water to get the bread down his throat. Ali was quiet throughout. He was patting Halima lightly on her back to keep her from crying but it didn't seem to be working.

"Why did you come back?",asked Ahmed once he was done.

"I found food",he replied.

"Mama will be back with more food"

Ali didn't reply to that.

"We need to find something for Halima to drink before Mama comes",said Ahmed

Ali nodded and then smiled. "I also got news"

"Mama's coming?",he asked with eyes full of hope.

Ali's smile faltered but he replied,"I heard from a man that this is all about to end. I heard it was something called a temporary truce. But it will stop Ahmed. They are not going to bomb us anymore"

"Are you sure?",asked Ahmed, his eyes glimmering with hope.

"Yes", replied Ali, grinning.

"We should find Mama and tell her the news",said Ahmed, getting up.

"Yeah",said Ali, not very hopeful and optimistic about finding Ahmed's mother.

"Let's go that way",Ahmed pointed. "That's where she went"

And they went on their futile journey to find Maryam.

CHAPTER THIRTY-FIVE

TAKING COVER

They searched for Maryam for about 2 hours before finally giving up.

"I think she lost her way and went the other way probably",said Ahmed, panting.

Ali didn't say anything because he didn't want to hurt Ahmed.

Ahmed got down on his knees and started crying. "Oh Allah give me a sign. Where is Mama.....Where did she go? Why did she leave us alone?"

Ali couldn't bear it anymore. He couldn't bear Ahmed thinking that Maryam had left them on purpose. He tried to calm down Halima crying in his arms, but she seemed to be very hungry.

"Ahmed",said Ali, sitting down beside him and having to speak louder so that he could hear him over Halima's cries. "When I went to search for food. I asked people about the line for food and that there was a woman who hadn't returned from there.....and....and they said that there was a drone strike on it...since it was a packed area there weren't many survivors..."

"No",Ahmed shook his head. "No it can't be.....it's not possible! Mama went to get food and she will be back with it. She survived. I know it. She must have been hurt, that's why she couldn't come back on time, but I know she survived."

"Ahmed, you're not listening, I'm -"

"Ali, please don't do this. She's my Mama, she can't leave me alone. I can't sleep without Mama. I can't -", his voice broke. "I can't live without her"

Ali chose not to say anything. "Follow me, I'll take you to the place where the line was attacked. Maybe she's there."

Ahmed, full of hope, started following him like an eager pet, following his master.

One minute later, Ahmed was on the floor, gasping for breath, not moving. It all happened so fast. They were walking and Ali was shot, possibly by a sniper. He had fallen with Halima and his beloved ball, in his arms. Ahmed was startled and he fell too, but he was too scared to move. Then he heard Halima crying loudly and he knew he had to get her to safety. Ali moved a little bit, which meant he was alive.

With tears welling up in his eyes, Ahmed started to get up. Another shot was fired, right beside Ahmed. He was being watched. That was a warning shot. The next would be put through his skull.

"Please! We're just trying to go find my Mama, please let us go", Ahmed shouted, making a futile attempt to change the mind of whoever was shooting at them.

They were kids, one with a single arm and the other carrying a baby. What danger did they possibly pose to a man with a gun?

Several men had gathered around, in a little distance, telling Ahmed to duck and take cover behind the giant rock a few feet away.

"Son, try coming this way",said the men trying to help him.

"My sister!",he called out to the men."My sister and my brother. I can't leave them."

His brother.

"They'll move their attention to a different person in a few minutes, we'll get them then, you get to safety right now. Raise your hand up, to show them you don't have anything and move to the side"

"No! Save them first. Please. Just get them behind the wall, I'll follow."

A brave man stepped up and with unwavering steps, he came towards Ali and lifted his bloody body up. He then took Halima into his arms and looked where the shots were being fired from. He looked at a distance with gaze as sharp as an eagle's and face so stoic it could be mistaken for a statue. Daring the person to shoot again. He then took them behind the wall.

Ahmed got up, following them, when another shot was fired, this time grazing his shirt. A few centimetres off and Ahmed would have been shot. The man was playing with him now. Ahmed immediately scampered behind the wall and sat there. The brave man still had Halima in his arms, but he had put Ali back on the ground.

Ahmed took a good look at his friend and he knew he wouldn't survive. His shirt was bloody and ruined. His eyes, spilling tears and his abdomen looked like it was about to be spilling his guts. Too much force used on a boy too small. Ahmed could see a gaping hole and he wanted to puke, but he couldn't do it infront of Ali.

"Call someone please. We need to take him to the hospital",said Ahmed, keeping his tears from escaping.

"The hospital was bombed, son. It is nothing but ruins now....and the other hospital is so far away that your friend won't survive the journey."

"Ahmed", whispered Ali, barely audible that Ahmed had to put his ear near his mouth. "Please don't leave me alone"

"I'm right here Ali. I am not going anywhere",he said.

"Take care of-",said Ali, then took a sharp breath. "Take care of my ball for me"

Ahmed smiled, "Ofcourse I will."

"Ahmed I'm scared",said Ali, his eyes half closed. Ahmed didn't say anything but he bit his lower lip to keep a sob from escaping.

"Ahmed", repeated Ali. "Ahmed the more I stayed with you, the more I feared death. But I can finally meet my family again. We can finally eat good food again."

Ahmed didnt say anything, he kept crying silently.

"Say something Ahmed", said Ali, tears coming out of his red eyes. "I never got to teach you how to play. Go- go find your Mama, Ahmed."

His words were becoming more strained by the minute.

"Sshh, repeat after me",said Ahmed, going near his ear and whispering. "*Ash-hadu an la ilaha illa Allah, Wa ash-hadu anna Muhammadar Rasulu-Allah*"

And the boy becomes a man.

Ali's face relaxed and his lips stretched into a faint smile. He repeated what Ahmed said and looked at him with grateful eyes. Thirty seconds and Ahmed heard Ali's last breath and saw his chest relax for the last time. Ahmed was almost jealous of him. He would get to meet his family as well as Ahmed's now. He was in a better place now.

Ahmed got up and took Halima from the man's arm. The man patted him on the back in a empathetic way but didn't say a word, he picked up Ali from the ground.
A few other men joined in, as they buried Ali.

"Come with me",said the man, after the burial. "I will find some food for you"
"My Mama's waiting for me",he replied.
"Where?"
"She's waiting for me, that's where we were going."
"Okay",said the man. "Be careful"
Ahmed went back the same route, carrying Halima in his arm. The man had helped him by tying a piece of cloth around his body so he could carry Halima with one arm, with ease.
He sat at place Ali had taken his last breaths and from behind the cover of the wall, Ahmed looked at the bloodied ball, placed in the middle of nothing and remembered how much Ali had loved that ball. But he couldn't go and take it. He could get shot.
"I'm sorry Ali"
He decided to take another route that led to where Ali might have been trying to take him.

CHAPTER THIRTY-SIX

REAL

Ahmed had questioned each and every person he could find, about his mother, but no one knew her. A man took him to a place where all the unidentified bodies were kept, from the bombing in the food line. And Ahmed couldn't recognise any one of them.

He was hungry, and tired. Halima kept crying but even she looked like she was out of tears now.

It was evening and Ahmed sat down, under a tree.

"We'll find something to eat Halima, don't worry. I won't....I won't let you die"

Even if Halima understood, it didn't matter to her, because the crying did not cease. Ahmed laid back his head and sighed. He heard footsteps, so he opened his eyes and saw his mother.

"Mama!",he cried happily. If he had the strength, he would have gotten up and hugged her, but he could even find the strength to lift his arm.

"How are you, Ahmed?",asked Maryam, looking at her son with morose eyes.

"I'm tired Mama. I can't do this anymore. I- I can't live like this anymore.",cried Ahmed, putting his head on her bosom. "Ali died. He died while he was trying to bring me to you."

"I know, son", whispered Maryam, you can pull through this, you're stronger than this.

Ahmed nodded and then said,"My arm and my shoulders hurt a lot. Can you please hold her."

Maryam looked at Halima and then back at Ahmed and whispered,"I can't"

"Why not?"

"Because I'm not here, Ahmed"

"What are you talking about?"

"You're making me up in your head, Ahmed. My presence here is a figment of your imagination."

"But I can touch you",said Ahmed in a low murmur.

"Ofcourse, because you're making me up in your head, Ahmed."

"You're real Mama",said Ahmed, now frantic with fear. "You're real to me"

"I'm dead Ahmed, accept it and move on like the brave boy you are now. Or should I say man?"

"But if I'm making you up in my head then how do I know you're dead. There's no proof you're dead."

"Yes there is. You visited that place with that man. You saw my body too, my face was burnt beyond recognition, but you recognised my arm, the same arm that fed you, the same arm that caressed your hair while you used to sleep soundly, the same arm that hugged and loved you. You saw my arms, you recognised them, you just didn't want to accept it."

Ahmed was silent. She was right. He had seen those arms.

"You didn't want to accept it, but your sub-consciousness wants you to realise it, Ahmed. We are dead, we have nothing to worry about. You and Halima are alive, so fight for the lives you have. Fight Ahmed, fight. She's your responsibility now."

"But I'm so tired Mama",said Ahmed, tears rolling down his face. "I just wanna go home. I just want to hug you one more time. I just want all this to be over Mama. Please take me with you"

"And it will be over, one day. Until then, fight my love. Halima is your responsibility now. Be the older brother she deserves.",Maryam smiled at him, her face red,"Now stop hallucinating and wake up Ahmed."

Ahmed looked around with a jolt and Maryam was gone. He was alone with Halima, who was still bawling.

"I won't let you die, my dear",said Ahmed in a hushed tone and got up despite his exhaustion, to find food for Halima. But first, he needed to bury his mother's body.

CHAPTER THIRTY-SEVEN

INTRODUCTIONS

Ahmed was impetuously searching for food in the trash. He couldn't find any other place to get food and maybe he could find something in the trash edible enough. He had eaten some grass, plucked out of the ground and now he was searching for something he could feed Halima.

He was on the verge of crying. When he was younger and used to see poor people searching for food in the trash, he used to feel sorry for them. He used to wonder how badly they must need the food that they were willing to go through literal trash to search for it.

Now Ahmed was doing the same thing and it made him want to cry out loud.

"Anything for my baby sister",he said to himself and kept on searching.

"You lost something?",came a voice and Ahmed looked up at a young man, wearing a ragged shirt, looking at him.

"I'm.... I'm looking for something to feed her",said Ahmed, looking at Halima, tied to his chest. "She hasn't eaten anything for a long time"

"She'll die",said the man

"Yes, that's why I'm searching for something-"

"No, I mean she'll die if you feed her something other than what she is supposed to be having. Milk."

Ahmed looked back and forth between Halima and the man, not able to decide what to say next.

"And....and where can I find that?"

The man looked serious and he gestured Ahmed to follow him.

Ahmed was extremely grateful to have met him.

The man took them to a tent where he was living with his wife. It had some essentials in store and some toys too, although Ahmed didn't see a child.

"They were for my son",said the man, with a smile on his face. "He's with *Allah*, now"

"*Inna Lillahi wa inna ilaihi ra'jioon*", whispered Ahmed.

"This is my wife, Aqsa",said man, pointing at the woman, then his focus went to Halima and his eyes softened."How are you two related?"

"She's my sister",said Ahmed, clutching her tightly to his chest.

"And your parents?"

Ahmed took a deep breath and then replied,"They're dead"

Before the man could say anything else, Ahmed started to explain what had happened. Not in details, but the facts did it.

And then the man turned his attention to his wife and started talking to her in a low voice. But Ahmed figured he was asking her to help Halima by feeding her. The woman agreed to it and the man asked Ahmed to give the weeping child to his wife so that she could feed her.

Ahmed was hesitant in handing over Halima to the unknown woman, but it was for her own good so he gave her up and followed the man out of the tent.

CHAPTER THIRTY-EIGHT

IBRAHIM AND AQSA

Ahmed found out that the name of the kind man and his wife were Ibrahim and Aqsa.

Aqsa reminded Ahmed of his mother, there was some resemblance in their features. She was a kind hearted person, just like her husband. She had helped in feeding Halima, for which Ahmed was very grateful to her. They had a son, Yousef, who had been murdered by a sniper, infront of them. And Ahmed noticed that while telling him this piece of information, Aqsa did not have sadness over her face, instead he saw a wave of pride pass over it.

"He is with the Martyrs now",she said. "He's with Allah, and nothing can harm him now."

It seemed to Ahmed that they were just biding their time until they were martyred too. They would happily accept their fate and meet their son. Ahmed yearned for the same type of feeling, where he could wish for death but he was the only family Halima had left, he couldn't give up hope. Not until *Allah* decided that it was time for him to rest.

Ibrahim entered the tent and told Ahmed to follow him, from where he took him to a long line for food.

"This is my spot. Just keep moving forward in line until it is your turn to take the food.",he instructed Ahmed, handing over a container to him. "When it is your turn, give them this container and they will fill it up. And from there, you'll bring it back to the tent. You understood?"

Ahmed nodded and then he noticed the man leaving so he asked,"Where are you going?"

"I need to collect some other necessities. I'll meet you back in the tent",said the man, going ahead.

Ahmed nodded again and silently stood there in line. He started reminiscing at how his father or Saleem, or his mother never made him stand in a line for food. He only ever ate it, not knowing what difficulty they had to go through to get the food. But they were not here anymore and he had to do things by himself now. Do things that he had never done before.

When it was his turn, he obediently handed over the container to the man, who filled it up and handed it back to Ahmed. It was not heavy for Ahmed to carry, even though he was carrying it with only one hand. There was barely enough food for two people.

He walked a little distance before toppling over and falling down. The bean curry, rice and bread in the container was all down in the ground now. Dirty.

Ahmed was petrified now. What was he to do. He immediately picked up the soiled bread from the ground and tried to gather the curry, but it was all ruined. Ahmed ran back to the line with his container, but they did not have any more food. Ahmed felt like crying. He felt like it was all just a nightmare.

"Why, *Allah*?", thought Ahmed to himself. "Why?"

When all of a sudden he felt a hand on his shoulder. He turned around and found a teenage boy standing there with his container.

"I saw you dropped your food",he said in a low voice. "I can give some of mine to you"

Ahmed was very grateful. "Thank you!"

He put forward his container and the boy poured down some curry. Another boy saw him and followed suit. The same boy called out to some other men, who happily gave a small part of their food into Ahmed's container.

"Thank you",Ahmed kept telling every person who shared.

And when it was done, Ahmed found that the container had become heavier. It had more food now than it initially did. This much amount of food was enough for three people. And Ahmed smiled all the way, carrying the container back to the tent. He was going to have proper food after so many days.

He looked up at the sky and his smile widened. "*Alhamdulillah*",he said, as he walked barefoot, wearing a ragged shirt, in a currently-being-bombed city, with one hand amputated and almost his entire family dead. "*Alhamdulillah*"

CHAPTER THIRTY-NINE

FAITH

Ahmed had been thinking about a question that he had heard a man asking a few children.

"If you could go back to the day it all started, what would be the one thing you would change?"

Ahmed kept thinking about it. His first thought was that he would prevent his family from leaving their home. They would have all gone down together. Ahmed remembered the day they were leaving their house, to look for Fatima. He remembered his mother packing up a bag and they were carrying stuff.

"Where is all that now?", wondered Ahmed.

Running for their lives, they must have abandoned it somewhere. He didn't even realise that he didn't have any personal object with him, except for his clothes and Halima.

"Ahmed, I'm going to the *masjid*. Come along",called out Ibrahim's voice. Ahmed followed him to a demolished *Masjid*. They had all gathered to pray beside the rubble. The enemy had broken their *masjid* but they couldn't shake their faith. A man was calling out for prayer while they all stood beside each other in rows.

"You know how to pray, right?",asked Ibrahim.

Ahmed frowned at him. What kind of a question was that?

"I meant with your hand and all..."

Ahmed nodded. "I manage"

They all started praying collectively. They were on the second *Rak'ah* when there was a loud sound nearby and packages were dropping from the air.

An aircraft was visible, dropping off food packages and essentials for them. It was what the people had been waiting for. The craft kept dropping the packages and some people were gathering around to collect it. But not a single person got up from the prayer. A testament of their strong faith. Ahmed could see the packages dropping from the corner of his eyes but he kept his eyes straight at where they were supposed to be.

"What if all the good packets are taken?",Ahmed let a stray thought form in his mind and he instantly waved it away.

"Prayer is more important",he convinced his mind to not sway.

Not a single person praying, got up to collect the packages in between the prayer. Only when they were collectively done, did they get up to do so.

CHAPTER FORTY

BRUNO

Ahmed was breaking down, by the side of the road. His water cart abandoned on the road. He had collected bottled water on a cart and tied the edge of the cart with a rope that he was pulling. It made his job easier, but the bumps on the road insisted on making it difficult and finally, a big hole, that Ahmed hadn't noticed, made him fall and hurt himself in the knee.

It was just a scrape. It was bleeding but it didn't hurt very much. Ahmed had instantly started crying and then he stopped after a few seconds. He realised there was no one to wipe his tears just then. No one to kiss his wound and pretend to hit and scold the ground for having hurt poor Ahmed. No one to clean up his wound or tell him to stop crying. His mother usually did that for him. But there was no mother around for him to run to.

He got up and pulled the cart to the tent. When he told Aqsa about his scrape, she inspected it, then applied cream and bandaged it up. She smiled at Ahmed and told him that it would be all fine. It was just a scrape.

Ahmed nodded,"Yes...it doesn't hurt much"

Aqsa tilted her head. "Then my dear why are you weeping so much."

"I.....I miss Mama and Baba.....I miss....I miss Saleem and Ali and....and Fatima..",said Ahmed, crying harder. "I miss them all so much."

Aqsa's eyes filled up with tears. "Oh my dear Ahmed, it will be alright. You will meet them one day *Insha Allah*"

She then proceeded to hug Ahmed.

Finally. Arms to cry into. Ahmed felt the warmth of a motherly hug after so long that it made him miss his mother even more.

She kissed Ahmed's head. "It will all be fine"

After a while, Ahmed had stopped crying and was playing with Halima, who was very giggly and happy for some reason. Ahmed made strange faces which made her giggle even more.

"Ahmed, did Ibrahim tell you where he was going?", asked Aqsa, who was sorting through the packet of essentials they had secured the day before.

Ahmed's heart fell with a thud. "Ibrahim is missing?"

"He hasn't come back. It's been 3 hours."

"I will....I will go check",said Ahmed getting up.

He dreaded going out and seeing Ibrahim, the man who had given him and sister, shelter and food, lying dead on the ground.

But after a few minutes worth of search, he found Ibrahim in perfectly fine state. As fine as a person can be, in an ongoing genocide.

"Aqsa",panted Ahmed, because he had been running. "She was worried you weren't coming back."

Ibrahim smiled a big smile. "I was going just there"

Ibrahim looked a little too happy, but Ahmed didn't ask why.

Ahmed realised that now his mind was set up in a way that whenever someone would go missing, he would immediately assume them to have been killed. He saw Ibrahim head towards the tent and his eyes went towards a destroyed shop and a man sitting infront of it with his hand on his head, facing the ground and drawing something on the dust.

Ahmed advanced towards the guy, hoping he was sane. "Are you okay uncle?",he asked.

The man looked up, he had big brown eyes, he smiled. "Ofcourse I am alright, child. My family is gone, my only source of income is gone but I am alright. I am A-okay. *Estoy Bien.*"

"Huh?"

"*Estoy Bien*, it means **I'm fine** in Spanish",the man explained.

"You know Spanish?",asked Ahmed amazed.

"A little bit", said the man getting up. "You know this was my shop. My toy shop"

"You have a toy shop?",asked Ahmed, even more amazed.

"Had, kid .....had a toy shop, now it's nothing but bricks, wood and half-burnt toys no one will buy"

"Why did they bomb a toy shop?"

"Even I was wondering the same thing, kid. But then I found out the truth",said the man, smiling, his eyes glimmering with playful mischief now.

"The truth is, that Bruno here, is a secret agent",said the man, still smiling, picked up a half burnt toy that he made out to be a panda. "Bruno was planning on overthrowing the Israeli government and they found out, so they bombed the shop, because that's where he lives. But no need to worry now, Bruno is dead. They succeeded."

Ahmed frowned at first and then he understood that he man was joking. It was all sarcasm and Ahmed laughed. He must have been a great salesmen. Creating back stories for his toys.

Ahmed heard a noise and they both looked to see something falling from the sky, in little parachutes.

"Food",said Ahmed happily.

"Food or bomb?",asked the man shrugging. "Who knows"

"Why would it be a bomb?",asked Ahmed, thinking the man was joking again.

"That's how my brother died",he replied."He opened a container thinking it was food or some necessary item and it blasted his face off."

"Why....why would they send bomb disguised as food?",asked Ahmed, now terrified.

"The same reason they would kill innocent civilians and babies and bomb a toy shop",said the man, looking away. "They were probably hoping for Bruno to be the one to open the container."

Ahmed realised he should be heading back now, so he turned around.

"They don't know we are all Bruno",the man called out as Ahmed was walking away.
That made Ahmed smile again.

"We're all Bruno",he smiled to himself as he headed back. .

CHAPTER FORTY-ONE

FIRST THINGS FIRST

Ahmed found out why Ibrahim had looked so happy when he had found him. He had discovered a way to get out of there. He told them that he had found a way to get all four of them out of there safely.

The news made Aqsa happy too, but Ahmed, not so much. For Ahmed it meant abandoning the place his family had died for. But he also knew that getting Halima out of there safely, was a priority too. He didn't tell them his thoughts.

Ibrahim found Ahmed sitting right outside the tent, staring up at the sky and at the rubble and dust that surrounded them as he sat down beside Ahmed.

"Aren't you happy?",he asked

"I am",said Ahmed, hesitantly. "Gaza is the only home I have ever known.....I don't feel good abandoning it...."

"We are not abandoning it. We are just saving our lives.",replied Ibrahim calmly.

"I know",replied Ahmed nodding. "I know"

They sat there in silence for another five minutes before Ahmed spoke again. "It used to be so beautiful."

"What?"

"Gaza.....this place. I remember coming to this area with Baba once. It was so full of life. Gaza was so beautiful you could write poems about it. It looked so beautiful.",said Ahmed, looking around. "Look at what they've done to our beautiful land."

The man looked up and sighed. "It's still beautiful. This is Palestine. It's beautiful even in sorrow."

Ahmed thought about it.

"Tomorrow we can leave. A friend of mine has gotten us a ride and from there, I will handle it.",said Ibrahim getting up. "We'll have to leave Ahmed. It's what is best for all of us"

Ahmed nodded quietly and said,"I know"

"And maybe when we are out of here, we can have that hand get looked at and get you a prosthetic one",said Ibrahim.

Hope. That's what Ahmed's eyes shone with.

"Really?"

Ibrahim smiled and nodded. "Yes Ahmed. But first we have to get out of here."

Ahmed sat there alone for some time silently. He felt very happy. He would get a new arm. He would be like other kids. He and Halima could go to school together. He started day dreaming about doing all the things he wasn't able to do.

But first things first, Ahmed thought. He wanted to get a toy for Halima. And then he remembered the man with the obliterated toy shop. Maybe he would be able to give one to him. The toy would be a reminder of his home land. It didn't matter if it was torn or a little burnt.

So he made his way to the desecrated toy shop, but the man wasn't there.

Ahmed was a little disappointed to not find him there. He couldn't take the toy without his permission. It would be called theft. So he turned around to go back when he found the man, looking at him with big eyes.

"You're back!",he announced happily.

"I....uh...I actually wanted to ask you if you could spare a toy",asked Ahmed, uncertainly.

"Well, which one do you want?",asked the man. "But I'll have you know, they're all injured."

"I actually don't have anything to pay with....so any toy could do",said Ahmed

"Well take your pick! It's fine. It's not like I'm going to sell them anyways. Look at their state",the man laughed.

Ahmed grinned and picked out a small soft toy, a turtle, with the flag of Palestine stitched on its back.

CHAPTER FORTY-TWO

BEAUTIFUL

Ahmed was admiring his turtle. It had its front limb a little burnt, which kind of reminded Ahmed of his own missing limb.

"It's perfect",said Ahmed happily.

"I'm glad you like it",the man smiled. "Take it"

"What is it called?",asked Ahmed

"Whatever you want it to be called. It's yours now"

"But....I can't think of any nice names"

"You didn't watch cartoons?"

"Sometimes",shrugged Ahmed.

"Well then, I'll suggest a name for him",the man put a finger on his chin and tapped it and then looked at Ahmed. "How about Jeremy?"

"Jeremy", repeated Ahmed looking at his turtle and then nodded. "I like it"

"That's good",said the man. "You can also take another toy if you want, there's this cute-"

There was an explosion that rocked the ground beneath Ahmed's feet.

They both looked at the source and saw dust and smoke around the left side.

"Another missile",said the man, sadly.

Ahmed's mind was racing. The smoke was coming from the area where his tent was.

"Halima",he thought and ran towards the source. People were running away but Ahmed was running towards it.

"Halima!",he screamed again."Aqsa! Ibrahim!"

No replies. They weren't nearby. That could only mean they were in the tent when it happened.

"Halimaaaa!",screamed Ahmed and ran towards where their tent was. It was just a dusty cloth and a few rods lying now. A few people were lying dead on the ground around it.

Ahmed moved the cloth and found three dead bodies. One of a child, another of a male and the last one, of a female.

He looked at the bodies of Halima, Ibrahim and Aqsa. He looked at them with eyes full of tears. His eyes stung. His chest was tightening up. He clutched the toy hard.

He knelt down beside Ibrahim's body. "You said we were gonna get out of here. You said I could get a new arm."

Ibrahim didn't respond.

He looked at Halima. Her legs were missing.

"Oh my baby",cried Ahmed, tears running down his shiny face. "Oh my baby. I'm sorry I wasn't here. I'm sorry I didn't protect you."

He kissed the top of Halima's dusty forehead.

"I'm sorry....Did you see Mama yet?"

He kissed her forehead again.

He put her body down gently and beside her body, he kept the toy he had gotten. She would have loved it.

He looked around and saw an armchair in the rubble there. Dusty and looking like it was almost going to break. He went ahead and sat on it. Tears still streaming down his face. His ears still ringing. He wiped those tears off his face and looked up at the horizon. Small objects were being from the sky.

"Food or bomb?", wondered Ahmed.

He looked around. Everything demolished. Everything ruined by people who had a talent of always doing the wrong things. Everything down on the ground. The last living member of his family, dead. Every feeling he had ever felt were fighting each other, wanting to be the first one to be expressed. Ahmed looked at the sky, glowing, the sun looking perfectly still and the clouds dancing around. Nothing could ever touch it.

But Ahmed knew his place. He knew he belonged there. In his homeland. And if he were to die, he would prefer to be murdered where his entire family had been murdered. In Gaza.

"Beautiful, even in sorrow",sighed Ahmed.

About The Author

Author Ramsha Rais, daughter of **Md. Rais** and **Shahnaz Salam,** was born on 11th February 2007. She lives in Kolkata, India. She was just 9 years old when she started writing stories and her first book was published when she was 13, called **Fired.** At 14, her second book **The door to the stars** and at 15, two of her books in a series **The Howling Alpha** got published. Now **Tears of the innocent** is her **fifth book** at the age of 17. She did her schooling from Saifee Hall, Park Lane. Her love for literature and writing is commendable. Tears of the Innocent was published by Notion Press on 29th July, 2024. She is also a World Record Holder.

E-mail address: raisramsha11@gmail.com

<u>RAMSHA RAIS</u>

www.ingramcontent.com/pod-product-compliance
Lightning Source LLC
Chambersburg PA
CBHW031151130726

47988CB00006B/2631